ONLY YOURS, ALPHA

EMILIA ROSE

Editing by: Jovana Shirley, Unforeseen Editing

Proofreading: Heart Full of Reads

Cover by: The Book Brander

Emilia Rose

emiliarosewriting@gmail.com

CHAPTER 1

AURORA

Shrill howls, ear-splitting cries, and monstrous growls echoed through the dense fog sitting over the Acheron River. I swallowed hard and inched even closer to Ares, my fingers intertwining with his and my heart pounding in my chest.

Charon stood at the head of the boat, using an oar to propel us forward. While his body remained stoic and *almost* poise, he turned his skeletal head a couple inches to the left and looked back at me, lifting his nose in the air and inhaling deeply.

"Charolette," he whispered, his words drifting out over the water.

Ares clutched my hand tighter. He glanced down at me, eyes a blazing gold, and clenched his jaw. *"Did he just say my sister's name?"* he asked me through the mind link, his entire body rigid.

I stared back at Charon, scared shitless but refusing to back down. *"Yes."*

As soon as I answered, the mind link went wild with our packmates wondering what he could want with someone like

Charolette—the woman we had left up on Earth to survive for us, the woman Marcel had come down here to save, the woman who would lead the rest of our pack.

We suddenly collided with the edge of a sleeping giant with red-pink skin, a single horn on the left side of his forehead, and teeth that resembled those of an orc. The boat teetered from side to side, some dirty water splashing over the edge and onto my feet, melting the slippers that I'd birthed my daughter in less than an hour ago.

Wrapping his skeletal hands around the wooden oar, Charon turned back to the front of the boat and gently pushed the oar into the side of the monster's ginormous belly to propel us back on our path.

The monster turned in the river, making more water spill into the boat, and sank deeper into his bath, bubbles emerging around him. None of my packmates, including Ares, said a word. I wasn't even sure if any of us had taken a breath since we'd stepped into the swaying boat, in fear we would alert the beasts who'd rip us to pieces and litter us in the water.

"I'm terrified," I admitted through the mind link to Ares.

We weren't ready for *any* of this. How would we know which monsters were friendly and which wanted to tear us to shreds? How would we pass all of them without being caught? Would we ever be able to get out of here alive?

Ares didn't respond, which meant that he must've been terrified too.

He clutched my hand harder and pressed his lips together in a tight line, and then he glanced down at me and gave my hand another squeeze. From down here, I could already see the anxious lines on his forehead, pulled together in a wary expression.

After swallowing hard, I glanced at Charon, who continued aimlessly rowing to the other side of the river through the fog. While I barely could see a few feet ahead of us, Charon must've been able to see farther. He must've done this thousands of times per day, millions per his lifetime.

Just like Ares and I knew the Sanguine Wilds like the backs of our hands, Charon knew this river so well that—now that he wasn't distracted by Charolette, nor her scent—he easily swept the boat past monster after monster, not colliding even once with them.

With every monster we passed, my heart pounded harder and harder inside my chest. My breath hitched, and I just wanted this damn ride to be over already. Bile rose in my throat. I didn't want to be here.

I wanted to be in the Sanguine Wilds with my baby.

Remembering the way Medusa—my own lousy mother—had snatched my daughter right from between my legs and run away from me without letting me see her, I balled my hands into fists and tried desperately to hold back the hot tears threatening to spill from my eyes.

But it had barely been a half hour since I had given birth, and I … I … I just wanted my child.

I held a hand over my empty stomach and bit back a sob.

My baby was gone.

And if I didn't keep quiet, these monsters in the water would awaken, and soon, I would be gone too. While we might've ruled the forest on Earth, down in the underworld, we'd merely be tasty monster food.

Ares wrapped his arms around my shoulders and pulled me closer, placing a kiss on my forehead and gently rubbing my shoulders. *"It's going to be okay. We're going to end this, and then we're going to see our girl again."*

"That's easy for you to say," I said, clutching him tightly. *"You were able to see her. I didn't even get a glimpse of her face, and I birthed her! I fucking birthed her, Ares. I don't know if I will ever forgive myself. How do I know who to fight for?"*

Instead of answering me, Ares stayed quiet. He was staying

positive *for me*, but none of this shit could be seen in a positive light, no matter how damn hard he tried. Medusa had stolen my baby from me and refused to let me see her, and then she'd banished me to the underworld for fuck knew how long.

Minerva moved closer to us and gently squeezed my arm. I glanced over my shoulder at her through watery eyes. While she wasn't one to smile much, she gave me her best smile that said she'd do everything in her power to get us back to the Sanguine Wilds.

"Your journey ends here," Charon said, his back turned to us.

Through the heavy moss and seaweed, the boat slowly drifted up to the other edge of the river and up onto solid land. He didn't step off the boat, but instead, he moved a couple inches to the side to let us off.

Wolves poured off the rowboat and onto the forest-covered land, engulfed in fog. I stood in the back of the boat and stared off into the woods, my stomach in knots. This might've resembled our home, but this was far from it.

Monsters and beasts roamed this land freely.

We weren't safe here. We weren't safe anywhere.

"Come on," Ares said to me, taking my hand and moving to the edge of the boat.

After he hopped off, he grasped both my hands to help me off too. But Charon had other plans, as he placed the oar between Ares and me, trapping me on the boat with him. My hands broke from our grip, and I snapped my head up at Charon, suddenly becoming the woman Mom had never let me be.

The alpha.

Or maybe this was the goddess side of me.

I was ready to fight him if he provoked me.

"Charolette," Charon said, staring down at me through his cold black eyes, "safe?"

Taken aback, I stared at him in confusion for a couple moments until he repeated his words again. Finally, I nodded and said them back to him, unsure of how he knew Charolette or why he wanted to know she was safe.

But as soon as the words left my mouth, he let me off the boat.

I hopped off into Ares's arms and turned around to see Charon already pulling the boat off the shore to row back to the other side. The boat and Charon disappeared through the thick fog, and my stomach turned.

"This way," Minerva said to the group, heading through the thick brush. "There looks to be a barrier or gate about a mile ahead."

We walked toward the black metal gate for five minutes without being ambushed by any undead monsters. It towered at least fifty meters above us and spanned out for miles upon miles. While it looked to be a door that we could walk through, there wasn't any doorknob.

"What do we do?" Minerva asked.

Feeling uneasy, I stepped back and closed my eyes. This was the gate into the underworld. Once we crossed it, there really wasn't any getting back. We would be stuck here for hundreds or thousands of years.

"I promised to fight forever to get back to you," I whispered to myself, gently rubbing my empty stomach.

My baby wasn't inside me anymore—she was somewhere in the world above—but I would never stop fighting to make it back to her.

She was my only hope that I would have in this darkness.

Suddenly, from above, a monstrous dog with three heads stood on the top of the gate and growled down upon us, warm spit dripping from each foaming mouth. He roared again and leaped down to our side of the gate and between my packmates, baring his teeth.

Cerberus.

CHAPTER 2

ARES

"Don't provoke him," I commanded the wolves behind me.

Cerberus towered over all of us, standing nearly three times taller than I did in my wolf form and foaming at all three mouths. We stared up at him, none of us saying a single word. Honestly, I didn't know what to say myself.

Venus had told us not to fear him, that he wouldn't hurt us.

And I knew that we could easily defeat him—because it was hundreds of wolves against one three-headed guard dog. It'd be easy to take him down, but then we would alert the rest of the gods as well as Hades himself.

Aurora sucked in a deep breath and stepped forward, staring the dog right in the face. He lunged at her quickly, but Aurora didn't even move a muscle. She stood rigidly before him and held the strongest eye contact I had ever seen from her.

Cerberus breathed at her neck with all three heads, his saliva dripping onto her shoulder. Hesitantly, Aurora lifted her hand,

and I desperately wanted to pull her back and away from the beast. But from the way she stood, I could tell that she didn't want me to do that.

Instead of swatting Cerberus, Aurora placed her hand on one of his snouts and gently stroked his fur. "We would like entrance into the underworld. We have some business here with gods and goddesses. Will you please let us enter?"

To my surprise, Cerberus tilted his head to the side, so Aurora scratched the side of his neck. Dropping his facade, he sat down in front of the gate and stared up at Aurora, wanting her to pet him more and more.

Aurora let out a heavy breath, shoulders slumping forward, as if she were relieved. "We're here to see Hades too. Can you point us in the direction of his kingdom? We've been informed that it's close."

Cerberus smiled—fucking smiled—at Aurora. After a couple moments, he nodded all three heads, stood back up, and pushed his paw against the gate, forcing it to open for him. The stone parted down the center, revealing a world of fog and woods and monsters.

"Thank you," Aurora said, giving him one last pet. She nodded for us to go through the gate to the other side. "I'll be back to see you again. I promise, Cerberus. I've missed you, boy. I have to make up for lost time."

Once we made it through the gate, Cerberus howled and closed it behind us.

Aurora smiled at me and nodded to the west. "Hades's kingdom is that way."

"You understood him?" I asked her, amazed.

"Yes," she said. "And I remember him too. It seems like I can remember almost all of the wolves and creatures that I've come in contact with in my past life. Cerberus helped us in the past. He saved us from trouble over a thousand years ago."

"Let's go before it starts to get dark," Minerva said, heading toward Hades's kingdom. "We should cover as much area as possible and try to find shelter for the night."

I led us through the forest and toward the kingdom that Cerberus must've pointed out to Aurora. But fifty meters into the underworld, I paused and grabbed Aurora's hand to stop her too. The wolves halted behind me, glancing around the densely foggy forest, almost as if they noticed or sensed someone watching us too.

"Stay behind me," I said to Aurora.

The innate need to prove myself to Aurora made my body swell with power. I'd vowed to protect her in every life. She wouldn't die like she had in my nightmares. This time, I would protect her and find Mars. We were so close to seeing him again.

I couldn't let him down, either.

Instead of following orders, Aurora stepped by my side and stood tall near me with her head held high and the colors of dawn in her eyes. Like I'd expected. My mate wasn't one to back down from a fight, not even when she had been pregnant.

"We're doing this together," Aurora said. "We're mates."

A growl rumbled through the eerie wooden area, then another, and then even another. Shadows ran from tree to tree, red eyes piercing through the thick fog. From every angle, they stared at us and lowered into their fighting positions, the way hounds always did on Earth.

"We're going to fight," I announced to my warriors. "To see our families again. To protect the wolves weaker than us. To survive down here. To end this madness once and for fucking all. No enemy hounds survive. We kill them all."

"Unless they're not aggressive," Aurora said. "Some of these hounds are rogues, forced down here during the War of the Lycans. They could be our ancestors. If they're not aggressive, don't kill them. But if they are, end their reign."

Together, the hounds roared around us, growing more and more restless. I lowered onto all fours and shifted into my wolf beside Aurora, who shifted right after me and brushed her snout against my side, as if to say that she was ready to fight for us and for our pup.

Then, in an uproar of paws pounding against the forest floor, the hounds raced toward us.

CHAPTER 3

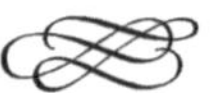

AURORA

*B*lood sprayed everywhere, drenching the forest floor and creating puddles of bodily fluids across the entrance of the underworld. Some hounds were stronger and physically bigger than the others, towering over them and powerfully striking us back. While others were weaker and fought slowly, like the rogues had the other day.

Almost as if they had come down here during the War of the Lycans.

Maybe they were rogues from Earth.

One hound sprinted at me with his bloody canines bared and dripping with thick saliva. He lunged at my stomach to rip it to shreds, but I quickly flipped him over onto his back and sank my claws into his throat, ripping it out easily.

With my paws coated in blood, I turned and tore another hound off a man that I didn't recognize from another pack. He cried out in pain and clutched his stomach, blood gushing out of his injury.

When I went to drop to my knees to heal him, one hound knocked me on my ass from the side, and another ripped the poor boy's head right off his body. I screamed in terror, the sound echoing through the forest. I had never seen a hound so strong.

Ares roared in response, sprinting over to me and taking the hound on, one-on-one. Similar in height and strength and muscle, they faced off head-to-head, tearing and ripping into each other's flesh so quickly that I could barely see straight.

My stomach tightened at the thought of this hound tearing my mate's head right off, and when they suddenly slowed down, Ares caught him in the throat and ripped his canine tooth across it horizontally.

The hound fell to the ground, twitching and shivering, foaming at the mouth and pissing himself. I stared at Ares with fear in my eyes and pain in my stomach. God, we hadn't even been down here for a few moments, and these hounds were stronger than expected.

Could we really do this?

Could we really survive?

When the hound finally stilled, the other weaker hounds stopped fighting too. It was as if that one had controlled them. And now, they all seemed to turn to me and the wolf who had knocked me back.

He was now lying on his back in front of me with blood pouring from a stomach wound.

Had I done that?

Though the hounds didn't shift, their wolfish whispers drifted through the air like a symphony. *"Dawn is here. Dawn is back. Dawn will save us."* They stared at me and then at the wolf under me, suddenly rushing through the woods and away from us.

"Dawn!" the wolf under me called to the others who were racing away, his voice fading. *"Tell Mars that Dawn is here."*

My heart pounded, and I grasped the hound's snout, gently

stroking his matted fur, desperate for answers about Mars's whereabouts. We had been without him for far too long, and he knew where he was.

"Tell me where Mars is, please," I whispered, tears filling my eyes.

The wolf parted his mouth and stared up at me, speaking words that were far too low and quiet and hoarse to understand. The light faded from his eyes quickly, his piercing golden eyes glazing over.

"Please," I cried frantically. "Please, tell me."

I pleaded. I begged. I needed answers.

But the more the wolf tried to talk, the quicker the life faded from his body. I stared at him, shaking my head and letting the tears stream down my cheeks. I didn't just feel bad for not finding Mars through him, but seeing a wolf that I used to live with dying in my arms...

The sight did something terrible to me. Absolutely terrible.

"Does anyone have any equipment to save him?" I asked, frantically glancing around at the others behind me.

Half of these people didn't even want to be here, hadn't thought that they were traveling to the underworld today, thanks to Medusa. Of course, they probably didn't have anything.

"Please," I said, holding the wolf in my arms. "Anything."

"He's a hound," someone said from behind me.

"He's a rogue," I said through clenched teeth.

When nobody emerged from the crowd, I cursed to myself and closed my eyes, trying desperately to summon the power I had inside me. Last time I'd tried while thinking about it, I couldn't heal Charolette. This time, I freaking hoped that I could do something.

We needed him alive.

I rested my hands on his wound and blew out a deep breath, focusing on his wounds closing and healing, imagining giving this rogue life once more. He deserved to leave this underworld for good one day and get back to his pack.

"It's working," a wolf said in the group. "Keep going."

Soon, the other wolves whispered around us, urging me to continue to heal him. A young woman that I hadn't met before emerged through the crowd, tearing off a piece of her shirt, large enough to wrap around the wolf's wound to hold it closed.

"Here, Alpha Aurora," she said to me, her cheeks a rosy red and her brown eyes wide. "We don't want you using all your power within the first few hours here. Use this to hold his wound closed. I have some herbs to stop the pain when he awakens."

Glancing up at her, I thanked the young woman—vowing to remember that I needed to ask her name once this was all over—and grabbed the cloth from her, wrapping it around the rogue's stomach to hold the remainder of his wound closed, hoping that it would stave off infection.

A couple moments passed, and I could feel his slight pulse. He blinked his eyes open a few times to stare up at me. When he opened his mouth again, he said, "Mars is at the ga—"

Before he could finish, a half-woman, half-bird creature with large brown wings and a beautiful face swooped down from the high trees. She pushed me out of the way and snatched the rogue wolf in her talons, lifting him off the ground and flying into the air.

"Hey!" I shouted, standing. "Where are you taking him?!"

She looked back at me with piercing red eyes, her wings still flapping in the air and taking her farther and farther from the pack. I was sure that I had never once seen this woman in this lifetime, nor my other lifetime either.

But she stared back at me as if she knew all my secrets.

"I'm taking him back," she said and then disappeared into the fog. "He's mine."

CHAPTER 4

ARES

*A*fter that beast woman swept down and grabbed the wolf from Aurora's arms, I took Aurora's hand and lifted her to her feet, glancing around the strange forest to see if anyone else was watching us. Something felt off.

My gaze focused on a flock of those half-woman, half-bird creatures, who stared at us from the highest trees in the forest, their beady red eyes narrowed at us and their feathers covering their mouths, as if they were gossiping.

Hands balling into fists, I let out a ferocious growl so loud that the trees and branches shook. Adrenaline pumped through my system, and I refused to cower back. Creatures in the underworld might've been terrifying, but I had a mate and pack to protect.

The flock took flight and followed the woman through the air and away from here.

"Come," Minerva said to us, pulling me out of my trance and nodding to the woods a bit farther ahead. "It's getting dark, and there looks to be a cave we can sleep in for tonight. We'll need to have some people keep watch and take turns sleeping and patrolling."

I tightened my hand around Aurora's and walked to the head of the pack with Minerva, scanning the woods to ensure nobody else would rush out and attack us. It might've been fucking insane, but that bitch Nyx seemed like she had eyes everywhere.

When we reached the cave, some warriors swept around it, so we weren't inhabiting another monster's home for the night and wake up, wrapped up in silk from a giant spider or as bear food. Who the fuck knew what went on down here?

"You can take the first shift to sleep," Minerva said to me and Aurora. She glanced down at Aurora's empty stomach and frowned. "You need rest. I'll keep watch with my warriors and wake you both up if someone attacks."

Once I thanked her, I sat against the cave wall and laid Aurora in my arms. This was a shit place to lie down for the night, the rock behind me hard as fuck against my back, but I wasn't going to let Aurora lie down on something like this.

She curled up in my lap and gave me her best smile, but it didn't reach her watery eyes. She had been trying to hold back tears all day, and I hated seeing her like this. I just fucking prayed to the Moon Goddess that we'd be back to Earth soon enough.

"I love you," she whispered, lifting her head slightly to kiss me on the mouth. "So much."

"I love you too," I said, gently caressing her cheek. "Now, get some sleep. You need it."

After settling into my arms, she closed her eyes and, to my surprise, easily fell asleep a couple moments later. Snores drifted through the air, and her body twisted and turned. She rested her hands on her stomach, as if our daughter were still in her belly.

Ruffles and the kittens curled up beside me in a bundle of fur, purring and licking each other. I laid a hand over Aurora's hands on her stomach and tried to still her trembling body, closing my eyes myself to get some sleep.

"I can't never see her again," Aurora mumbled, tears sliding down her cheeks.

I opened my eyes briefly and wiped her tears away, one by one, and held her closer to me, so she wouldn't shake in these unknown lands. Not only did I not want anyone, especially Nyx, to see her this sensitive, but I also didn't want her to hurt anymore.

We were going to fix this.

Still, I couldn't help but feel helpless because I couldn't do anything to soothe her.

Maybe that was what came along with being the god of war.

I wasn't always strong. I just acted that way because I didn't want anyone to feel the way I did every night. I wanted people to be secure and safe and without these fucking nightmares plaguing their minds daily.

One day, I would be strong enough.

* * *

AN ALMOST-ANGELIC LAUGH echoed through the pack house.

Our daughter sat on my lap, her small body fixed on my knee and her face nothing but a blank, pale slate. No eyes, no nose, no lips, no features. Nothing but a cruel, horrid sight. And while I thought that this was my own nightmare, I knew that it wasn't.

I had seen our daughter's face. I knew what she looked like.

But Aurora hadn't.

She hadn't seen our girl, and part of me thought that I didn't remember her the way she really was. But unlike the last time I had seen her, her body was a bit bigger, almost as if she were a toddler. And my lap wasn't mine at all; it was Vulcan's.

He smiled down at my daughter like she was his own while holding another baby on his lap, who seemed to be around the same age. He ruffled his hair and grinned. "You're going to take care of our pack and your sister one day, aren't you, Kairo?"

The boy grinned and reached for my daughter. He gently patted her head and giggled. Vulcan placed Kairo and our daughter on the ground, letting them crawl and stumble to the blocks and figures of wolves and monsters.

"It's been years," Venus whispered to him, shaking her head and grimacing at the kids. "I fear that Ares and Aurora aren't coming back, that they'll never get to see their daughter again. I fear they're trapped there, like I told Medusa they would be."

"You worry too much," Vulcan said to her, curling his arm around her waist and smiling.

"No," she said. "You don't understand how it is down there."

"Please, just relax for a moment, love. They'll be back."

Venus pulled herself away from him and shook her head, tears filling her eyes. "No, they won't. They'll never see their daughter again. I've heard a rumor that Medusa didn't even let Aurora see her baby. How could she?"

"No!" someone screamed from beside me, but neither Venus nor Vulcan heard.

I glanced over to see Aurora beside me, banging on an invisible wall to run into the nightmare and take her child back for herself. She banged violently, but never broke the barrier into the dream.

Suddenly, she turned toward me.

"I can't never see her again, Ares," she cried. "I can't never see my baby."

CHAPTER 5

MARS

*A*n almost-angelic laugh echoed through the pack house.

A young girl sat on Vulcan's lap, her small body fixed on his knee and her face nothing but a blank, pale slate. No eyes, no nose, no lips, no features. But something about her reminded me of Aurora.

I hadn't seen our daughter, but I knew that this was her.

Vulcan smiled down at my daughter like she was his own while holding another baby on his lap, who seemed to be around the same age. He ruffled his hair and grinned. "You're going to take care of our pack and your sister one day, aren't you, Kairo?"

Sister? Our daughter isn't Kairo's sister unless ... unless Aurora has had another baby without me. But why is Vulcan watching them? Where is my Aurora and my other half, Ares? Have they gone missing? Gotten killed?

The boy grinned and reached for my daughter. He gently patted her head and giggled. Vulcan placed Kairo and our daughter on the ground, letting them crawl and stumble to the blocks and figures of wolves and monsters.

"It's been years," another goddess said to him, shaking her head and grimacing at the kids. "I fear that Ares and Aurora aren't coming back, that they'll never get to see their daughter again. I fear they're trapped there, like I told Medusa they would be."

My chest tightened. Where did Aurora and Ares go? Why did they leave our daughter?

"You worry too much," Vulcan said to her, curling his arm around her waist and smiling.

"No," the goddess said. "You don't understand how it is down there."

"Please, just relax for a moment, love. They'll be back."

She pulled herself away from him and shook her head, tears filling her eyes. "No, they won't. They'll never see their daughter again. I've heard a rumor that Medusa didn't even let Aurora see her baby after she was born. How could she?"

"No!" someone screamed from beside me, but neither Venus nor Vulcan heard.

I glanced over to see Aurora, my beautiful mate, beside me, banging on an invisible wall to run into the nightmare and take her child back for herself. She banged profusely, never breaking the barrier into the dream.

Suddenly, she turned toward me.

"I can't never see her again, Mars," she cried. "I can't never see my baby."

JOLTING AWAKE, I sat up in the bed of my one-bedroom cottage between Nyx's kingdom and Hades's kingdom. My stomach twisted and turned from the horrid dream that I had experienced, and I glanced over at the painting Apollo had created for me almost a hundred years ago now.

It was of the last moment I had seen Aurora with the image of what I thought our baby would look like. It might've been over a century since I had laid my eyes upon her, but she never left my mind. Her image was always crystal clear.

I drew my fingers across the painting and smiled down at her, like I remembered doing long ago. She always had the most beautiful, piercing eyes in the morning, so soft and delicate, so loving when they glanced over at me.

My chest tightened, and I leaned over the side of my bed, vowing that someday soon, I would get to see her too. Everything that I did down here, I did for her. And I knew that Ares was taking care of her the way I had.

Even though it had been a hundred years since I had seen her, time worked differently down here for individual species. For some, time moved slower than it did on Earth. For others, like spirits like me, time moved faster than it did on Earth.

For all I knew, Aurora might not have even had our child yet.

It didn't matter, though. I still vowed to see her and our child one day.

Once I shook away last night's nightmare, I stood and padded through the small cottage to the makeshift kitchen and glanced out the window. Wolves gathered outside my house, pacing around the front and howling for me to come outside—the way they always did when they had important information for me about the war happening between the wolves and Nyx.

I peeked outside the window again and furrowed my brows.

Except these weren't the wolves that I fought with. They were Nyx's wolves.

Lengthening my nails into sharp claws, I unlocked my door and stepped outside, ready to fight by myself if they became violent. It wasn't like them to show up to my house, especially at this hour. Hell, I hadn't even thought they knew where I lived.

While they didn't shift into humans—they were trapped as wolves down here—one walked up to me and lay down at my feet, the haziness in his eyes completely gone but wounds deeper than I had ever seen them.

I crouched down and hesitantly brushed my fingers across his fur.

These wounds hadn't been inflicted by any monster down here. These had been done by werewolves.

The wolves paced around me unsteadily and nervously, none of them saying anything to me yet. I had fought them before, but now, they weren't harming me and were actually being a bit too calm.

"What is it?" I asked.

"Dawn," the wolf barked, voice throaty and dry. "Dawn is here."

"Dawn, as in Aurora?" I whispered.

Instead of answering me verbally, he nodded. I scooped the wolf into my arms and ran into my home to gather the healing supplies that I'd stolen from Nyx's kingdom. After laying the wolf on my stone floor, the other wolves followed me into the room and lay by his side.

I rummaged through the supplies to find healing powder and bandages, and then I worked quickly to heal the poor creature who Nyx and Hella must've been torturing these past few years. These wounds might've been done by werewolves from above—Aurora maybe—but these wolves had only fought them because Nyx had told them to hunt her.

But what I couldn't wrap my mind around was why he had said Aurora was here.

Why had she come here?

Once I placed the final bandage over his fur to hold his wound closed, I heard a howl of wolves in the distance. My entire body tensed, as I recognized the sound as Nyx's army. Over the years, I had heard that sound many times.

It had been followed by nothing but war, death, and disease.

And with a weakened wolf lying in my house, I couldn't fight.

I needed to abandon this place for good to meet up with the other wolves, the other gods, and someday, my family again. So, I grabbed the painting of Aurora, stuffed it into a string backpack, picked up the wounded wolf, and ran with the others in the opposite direction.

Ares would be disappointed that I had run from this battle, but I didn't have his skill. He hadn't been down here for a hundred years, wondering how his mate was doing and if their baby had made it into the world.

I would survive to see them again.

CHAPTER 6

AURORA

*A*fter that horrible nightmare, I walked next to Ares toward Hades's kingdom. I had tossed and turned all night, and then I'd needed to awake to stand guard with my pack while the others slept. To say I hadn't gotten any sleep was an understatement.

Yawning, I wiped my tired eyes and listened to the quiet morning hum in the underworld. Warriors scanned the woods for other hellhounds and hounds who might try to attack us. I continued forward and hoped that we'd get some information on the hounds, Nyx, and maybe even Mars's whereabouts at Hades's place.

"There is a castle about a half mile ahead," Minerva announced. "Let's hurry."

I picked up my pace, wanting to get out of these woods as quickly as possible. Sometime during our walk over here, the thick mist had turned to darkness up above—or maybe the trees were just too thick to let any light through.

Those bird ladies who had taken the wolf from me yesterday were perched on high trees, staring down at us. Their beady and narrowed eyes almost sparkled in the darkness that swarmed us from above.

"They're called harpies." The same woman from yesterday who had helped heal that wolf stepped toward me while we walked. "I've read about them since I was a child, but I didn't think that they were real. They try to abduct people heading toward Hades's kingdom."

"Stay close," Ares growled to the group of warriors and headed toward the front with Minerva to inform her. "Don't let those assholes take another."

"What's your name?" I asked the young woman.

"I'm Acesca."

"I'm Aurora."

"Oh, I know." She smiled. "I've admired you for so long. I can't believe I'm talking to you."

Though I didn't have much to smile for anymore—except Ares—I found myself smiling. All this time, I had been so focused on protecting my pack and the wolves above from the hounds, dealing with my back and the Malavite Stone, I never thought about how I might've affected other people.

"What pack are you from?" I asked.

"I'm from Vulcan's pack." She wrapped her arms around her body and frowned. "I wasn't even supposed to be here with you all. Medusa asked me to come to the goodbye get-together yesterday morning to aid you while giving birth."

My stomach tightened, and I stared at the ground. *To help me give birth? Does that mean Medusa had planned for me to give birth during that time? Did she expect it? Maybe she'd foreseen it in a vision or something...*

Still, that didn't explain why Acesca hadn't been with me while I gave birth. If Medusa had asked her to come to the goodbye ceremony, then why hadn't she called Acesca into the room while I was giving birth?

Acesca's gaze dropped to my stomach. "But I see that has already happened."

"Yeah," I whispered, refusing to cry over it again, but *fuck* had I been hormonal lately. "It did."

As we reached the end of the thick forest, Minerva and Ares suddenly stopped along with the rest of the warriors. I pushed through the crowd to get to the front and stopped dead in my tracks.

Ghostlike creatures, their bodies wispy and almost transparent, wandered around Hades's kingdom aimlessly. Some of the older creatures had blurry features like feet and hands, their details harder to make out.

Except one.

Arms moving back and forth, he strode forward quickly, heading straight for the doors to the castle. With a body like his, I expected him to be able to walk right through the other ghosts, but he avoided them entirely.

It was almost as if people like this were still solid human beings.

But then, when he reached the top step, he disappeared right through the door without opening it, without transforming his body. He just stepped right through it and disappeared from the outside forever.

I frowned, hoping that Mars wasn't like this. If he had died, if these people were thoughtless bodies who'd died on Earth ... then was that what Mars looked like now?

"Kitten," Ares said, grabbing my hand and pulling me away from the path of one of the walking ghosts.

While I hoped that Mars wasn't like the man who had disappeared through the door, I really hoped that he wasn't like the ones walking around mindlessly. I hoped that he was still waiting for me, that he still had a mind of his own, that he could make his own decisions, and that he would remember me, Ares, and our little girl.

"Come on." Ares tugged me along and toward the castle. "We need answers now."

Being careful to avoid the creatures, we walked around them and up the path toward the castle. Before we could knock on the grand obsidian doors, someone pulled them both open and stood before us.

A handsome man, as tall as Ares but much skinnier, cleared his throat and smiled at us. "Ares and Dawn, welcome. We've been waiting for your return. In case you don't remember me, I'm Hades, king of the underworld."

CHAPTER 7

ARES

*H*ades stepped back into his castle and held one of the doors open for us to enter. I grabbed Aurora's hand, wanting her to stay close, and pulled her into the castle with the rest of our warriors.

A ghostlike man with striking features paced the foyer, muttering to himself.

"We will—"

"Hella and Nyx have pushed the gods back even further," the ghost said to Hades, completely interrupting him, his hands running through his hair every now and again. "I fear they'll trap them soon within their borders and won't ever let them leave."

"We will handle it. We have reinforcements now," Hades said, glancing at us.

"It's not only that. They are also—"

"Phobo, please, let me welcome our visitors."

After Phobo disappeared down the hallway, muttering and cursing to himself, fear plaguing every one of his features, Hades glanced down at Aurora's belly, like everyone had been doing lately, and frowned.

"I'm sorry for your loss, Dawn. Medusa told me what she did to you and your family. I can feel the pain that you're in."

Instead of responding, Aurora pursed her lips together and placed a hand on her belly. "We need information."

"Of course." He walked into another room with a long table fit to seat hundreds of people. "The other gods have been waiting for your return. You're welcome to stay with me for as long as you need, but I suspect that you'll want to get out there and fight with them."

"How are the gods fighting?" I asked.

"They've been losing the war since you left." Hades sat at the head of the table and gestured for the rest of us to sit too. "I doubt you remember everything that happened during your time fighting in the underworld with them. Medusa mentioned that you have scattered memories. But truthfully, we've never been winning. They have powers to kill gods."

"We're losing, but not for long," someone said, strolling into the room with a lyre in his hand. He walked right up to my mate and slung his arm around her shoulders, smiling down at her. "It's been a long time, Dawn. You're going to change this world for good this time."

Aurora glanced up at me, and I couldn't hold back a growl. "Get your hands off her. She's mine."

"Apologies." He pulled his arm away. "Medusa was right. It seems you don't remember me or much down here. I've been watching you since you entered the underworld. I'm Apollo, one of the gods who's been trapped in this *hell*, distantly related to Dawn or … Aurora, as you call her."

Whether they were related or not, I didn't care. I pulled my mate closer.

"Dawn, I actually have something for you," Apollo said, unstrapping his pack and pulling out a large notebook. He tore out a piece of paper. "Usually, I prefer music and poetry, but I do enjoy painting the beauty of gods and goddesses."

Apollo handed Aurora a painting with strong blue brush-strokes across the page. I glanced over her shoulder and examined the image that looked to be a copy of myself, except my body looked wispy and transparent, like those ghosts outside.

"A hundred years ago, Mars asked me to draw a photo of you." He gave a small smile and drew his fingers across the page. "I told him that if I ever saw you before he did, if I ever made my way to Earth again, I would give this one to you."

"A hundred years ago?" she whispered. "Mars has only been gone for a few weeks."

"Time works differently here for distinct beings," Hades announced to all the warriors scattered across the room. "You'll understand soon enough. The dead, undead, and living beings in the underworld age unusually as well."

"What does that mean for Mars?" she asked, glancing up at me through teary eyes.

"While it's only been a couple weeks for you, it has been a century for him."

A century ...

How has he survived down here all that time, alone?

"So, those creatures outside, those ... ghosts," I whispered, "they're the dead?"

"The simple answer, yes," Hades said.

Which meant that, if Apollo had drawn Mars that way, he'd actually died during that fight with Hella. I hadn't been fucking insane like Denise, that bitch therapist, had told me I was being. I was right, really and truly right.

I stared out the windows at the ghosts walking around in the underworld and unclenched my jaw. Maybe Mom was one of these many ghosts down here, wandering around aimlessly and thinking back to Charolette and me.

Will she remember me? Has Mars found her yet? Is he doing good down here?

A piercing pain shot through my chest, right over the fatal wound that had killed Mars. Just thinking about him brought back bad memories. And while I expected the memory and the hurt to fade quickly, it didn't.

It only intensified.

I clutched my chest, the pain bringing me to my knees, and grunted in hopes to displace the hurt. I didn't feel too much pain, but this was more than I'd ever experienced.

"Ares!" Aurora cried, hurrying over to me and kneeling by my side. "What's going on?"

"I'm fine," I said through gritted teeth.

Everyone in the room stared at me, including the other gods. And I didn't want to seem weak in front of anyone. We had to fucking show that we were here to fight, that we wouldn't succumb to the hounds like the other gods had. We were here to save the world.

When Aurora peeled my hand away from my chest, blood seeped through my shirt from the same fatal wound. I lifted my shirt to see the gash had reopened, but it looked like someone had sliced me through the chest perpendicular to the scar, like this was fresh.

"The hounds and gods are fighting again," Hades said, glancing at my wound and standing, suddenly worried. "We must prepare for them to run on my kingdom. They've been getting closer and closer to our gates. I'm not sure if Cerberus is strong enough to hold them back."

"Is Mars with them?" Aurora asked, hands still on my chest, using her power to keep the wound closed even though it kept reopening, almost as if I were being stabbed over and over again. "He has to be fighting with the gods, right?"

"Yes," Hades said. "Mars is fighting with them. If we hurry, you might get to see him."

CHAPTER 8

MARS

*P*ain shot through my body.

I grazed my fingers against the spear impaling my chest, right where the underworld gods had killed me the first time on Earth, and gritted my teeth to ignore the agony. After I pulled the spear from my chest, I glanced down at where the wound should've been, only seeing the molecule-like skin fizzle back and forth for a moment, as if the weapon weren't just lodged in my torso. It wasn't bleeding either.

Hella howled in front of me, screaming and shrieking. She grabbed another spear from fuck knew where and hurled it at me, becoming a wild and feral animal, just like the hounds she rose from the dead.

"I'm going to kill you for getting Dawn pregnant," Hella screamed. "You're mine!"

Swiftly, I ducked out of the way and grabbed the weapon right in the air, my hand wrapping around the handle like it was meant to be there. This spear felt like it belonged to me. I had never used a spear before, but … I grasped and aimed it like I had used it a thousand times.

Stepping forward, I threw the spear back at Hella and pierced her in the shoulder. The spear continued to fly back, pinning her to the closest tree. She let out a harrowing scream and grabbed her shoulder.

After struggling for a few moments, she removed it from her body and slumped to the ground. I picked up the spear she'd hit me with and lunged forward to send it flying through the air toward her.

This time, she moved out of the way and sprinted in the opposite direction, retreating with the hellhounds and undead wolves she had raised with Fenris. Since I had been down here, I hadn't seen him once.

I ached to follow her, but far too many wolves had died down here today. I walked around the battlefield and around them all, ready to regroup with the rest of the gods to come up with another plan on how to be on the offense, not defense anymore.

These attacks from her were almost daily now, and I didn't know how much longer I would be able to handle this shit. It had been years.

"Mars!" Flora shouted, hurrying toward me with a big smile. "You remember how to use a spear."

I walked past her and grabbed the spear from the tree, holding it in my hand. Memories flooded through my mind, thoughts that I couldn't quite piece together, but I knew that I had held this spear before and I had used it in many past wars and many to come.

She hurried after me and placed her hand on the center of my back. "It's amazing."

My entire body froze, and I pulled away from her, not liking how close she had been toward me lately. Every morning, she'd find me in the closest village or bring me vegetables that only grew in the underworld.

It was something that I could only imagine Aurora doing.

Like Flora was trying to replace my mate.

"Don't touch me," I said politely, walking toward the other gods with the spear in my hand and my thoughts on Aurora. If what that wolf had said was correct and truthful, then that meant Aurora was down here, looking for me. "Aurora is here."

"What?" Flora whispered from behind me. "What do you mean?"

"Aurora is in the underworld."

"Who told you that?" she said, almost with spite.

"Hella's wolves."

Flora let out a low laugh and shook her head. "Come on. You're going to believe them? Hella is just trying to fuck with you. She'll probably summon a demon that can shapeshift into any human, even Aurora, and then she'll kill her in front of you. Aurora will never come back for you, Mars. Not in the underworld," Flora said. "She's gone."

"You're wrong," I said, pulling out the picture that Apollo had made of her.

Fury ran over Flora's features, and she snapped the picture from my hand. "No, she's—"

Before she could say another word, I thrust her against the nearest tree so hard that it snapped, cracked, and fell in the woods. With my hand wrapped around her neck, I dug my claws into her skin and grabbed the art of Aurora from her fingers.

"Don't you dare fucking take this from me again," I growled. "Or I'll kill you myself."

Instead of dropping her head, nodding, and walking away, Flora clenched her jaw and shook her head, tears welling up in her eyes. "Why won't you understand? You're so hung up on her that you barely even look at anyone else. She's not coming back. And even if she did, you're dead, Mars. Dead!"

I loosened my grip on her throat and felt my arm fall to my side, those words ringing out through the now-quiet forest. I hadn't heard or thought those words in years now, almost half a century. But Flora was right.

Hella had killed me on Earth.

Even if Aurora came to the underworld, even if she was really here, how would she like someone like me? The longer that I lived in the underworld, the more transparent and essence-like my body became. Sometimes, if someone touched me, their hands would slip a few centimeters inside me. Someday, they'd be able to pass right through.

How would Aurora love someone like me? How could she?

We wouldn't be able to even touch.

My fingers curled around the drawing of Aurora that Apollo had made for me, and I frowned. One day, I might not even be able to touch this image. Aurora might be gone from me for good, and then I would have nothing to remind myself of her.

"Let her go," Flora said.

Hearing those words come out of her mouth, I growled and ripped myself away from her. "Stay away from me," I said through gritted teeth, turning on my heels and storming through the woods, where the other gods had disappeared.

She had come back down here for me, for us, for our daughter.

I refused to let Aurora go now. Not after I'd been waiting almost a century to see her again.

CHAPTER 9

AURORA

"They're retreating," Hades announced, stopping and watching the hellhounds sprinting in the opposite direction through the woods. He stuck the end of his bident on the ground and clenched his jaw. "They're leaving."

I watched the wolves run far away from here after we had destroyed about half of them with our strength, numbers, and magic. But it didn't make sense. They were alone, and it seemed like we had found them and cut them off, as if they were running somewhere to meet up with someone—maybe Hella.

"Mars isn't here," I announced, more for myself than for Hades or Apollo or even Ares. I walked through the dead hellhounds that we needed to kill in order to survive and frowned, not finding Mars anywhere. "Where is he?"

"They must've been fighting elsewhere," Minerva said, crouching by the wolves and running her fingers over one of their snouts. "We must've cut off these wolves from getting to Hella and fighting against the other gods."

"They're stronger than I ever imagined," Acesca muttered and wiped some blood off a warrior with her supplies. Then, she stood and walked over to me. She nudged me and glanced up at the trees. "The harpies are watching again."

I looked up at the bird-woman perched high in the trees and furrowed my brows, my stomach tightening. "We're with Hades and the other gods. What do you think they want? Don't they only take people who are traveling to Hades's kingdom?"

She chewed on the inside of her lip. "I'm not sure."

"Nobody knows what they want. They show up whenever they feel like it. But we should head back to the castle to regroup and form a plan," Hades announced. "We have much to talk about and even more to catch up on. So much has happened since you were killed the first time. And we can chat about Mars."

I glanced over at Ares and gave him a small smile. "We would love that."

So, I strolled alongside my mate back to Hades's castle. As we stepped onto his property and walked around those mindless ghostlike creatures, I glanced over at Apollo and let go of Ares's hand. I had a question, one that had been bothering me since Apollo had given me the picture of Mars.

I glanced over at Apollo and held my hand to my stomach. "I don't usually ask anyone for favors, but would you be able to draw my daughter? She was taken from me before I could even see her, and I want something to remember her by."

Apollo stopped before we entered Hades's palace. After taking a seat on a large rock, Apollo pulled out a notepad and sketch pen, as if he kept one on him at all times along with his lyre. "I won't ask what she looks like, but I'll make her how I believe any child you and Ares have together would look like."

Apollo whipped up a quick drawing of our daughter—or what he thought she'd look like—and handed it to me, his lips turned up into a small smile. I moved closer to Ares and grasped his hand, staring at the bright eyes of my daughter for the first time.

It was far from the real thing, but it was something.

I had never fucking seen her before. Not once.

"How does she look to you, Ares?" Apollo asked. "You've seen a glimpse of her."

Ares stayed quiet for a few moments, his eyes glossing over. "It's our daughter," he whispered, muscles tightening. "This is our daughter."

"How do you like it?" Apollo asked me.

"I love it," I whispered, bursting into tears and grasping the page so tightly.

Acesca moved beside me and gently rubbed my back, whispering that it would be okay. But I couldn't stop crying.

"I love it so much. I miss her."

Ares took me from Acesca and picked me up, cupping my face with his large, callous hands. "We're going to be okay. She's going to be okay. We're doing this to see her again, Aurora. You have to stay strong."

I balled his shirt in my fists and pulled him closer to me. "I miss her so much."

"Me too, Kitten," Ares whispered against my lips. "I miss her too."

"We need to find Mars," I said. "He needs to know that his daughter is okay."

"You can search for him at his home. He lives a few miles from here."

"He does?" I asked, perking up at the thought. "Why didn't you tell us earlier?"

"Because we needed to talk about more important things, like this war," Hades said.

Instead of addressing the war anymore today—because by the looks of it, they didn't have much information yet either—I grabbed Ares's hand and led my warriors to the door. "Come on. We have to go find him. He has to be close."

Hades nodded. "I knew that you would. Find his home and

then come back tonight, so we can chat. I want this to be over once and for all."

"Unfortunately, I'll be gone when you get back," Apollo said. "I have business with other gods, but I hope to see you again, Dawn. Our paths will surely cross once more. And if I see Helios, I'll let him know that you're here."

"If you find Mars before I do, can you give him this?" I asked, placing the drawing back in Apollo's hand and curling his fingers around it, desperate for him to take it before I tried to steal it back from him. Because I wanted to keep it so badly. "Please, show Mars who our daughter is."

Ares squeezed my free hand. "Are you sure, Kitten?"

"Yes," I whispered, pulling away from Apollo. "I want him to know that we're here for him, that we're going to find him, and that we'll bring him home, no matter who he has become or how he looks. We will be a family again."

ARES

"It should be nestled in the forest, right across that river," Aurora said, glancing at the map that Hades had drawn up for us before we left. She glanced into the river and stuck her toes in the water, wincing. After a couple moments, she hummed and looked down at her feet. "I expected it to hurt."

I grabbed her hand and glanced into the rushing river that separated Hades's kingdom from the rest of the underworld, and then I nodded to the warriors who'd decided to come with us to find Mars's home. Most were from our pack, but there were others here, like Acesca.

Taking Aurora in my arms, I lifted her into the air and stepped into the rushing water. My pack walked into the water with me until we were waist deep, pushing through the current until we reached the other side.

After I placed Aurora down on solid ground, she helped me out of the water and gave me a small smile. Through our mate bond, I could feel the fire and exhilaration rushing through her body. We were so close to seeing Mars again, so fucking close.

I could sense him somewhere in these woods.

"Come on," Aurora said, grabbing my hand and tugging me through the woods. Using the map to direct us, she walked around a small cliff and then swung around the curve of another river, finding her way through the trees. "We're close."

"He might not be there, Kitten," I said, not wanting her to get her hopes up.

But I was excited too.

It had been so long since he and I had been merged together. I was surprised that he had been down here for so long without me to protect him. It was my job to protect him and Aurora, and I wanted to be able to do that again as soon as possible.

Hurrying faster through the woods with me, Aurora suddenly stopped. "No."

I glanced around at the house settled under the thick trees and frowned, my heart and stomach dropping and a bad feeling rising in my throat. "It's in ruins," I said, squeezing her hand so she would know that she wasn't alone.

Aurora walked into the house, and I followed after her, not wanting anything to jump out at her and try to fucking eat her in here. Who knew what Hella must've left for Mars to come home to … if he was ever planning on coming back?

While it was a small cottage, only the living room seemed to be left. The bedroom and bathroom had been completely destroyed from the inside out, the walls broken down, as if a giant had stepped on it.

"There is blood on the floor." Aurora dropped down next to it. "Do you think he's okay?"

I sniffed the air to smell the blood. "It's not ours—I mean, *his.* This blood is one from those hellhounds."

"Aurora," Acesca said, hurrying into the room, grabbing her hand, and pulling her toward the front door, where the warriors had gathered and shifted into their wolves, as if they were ready to attack. "The harpies are here."

"The harpies?" Aurora said breathily. "Why?"

I hurried past them and through the group of warriors, spotting a flock of those bird creatures perched on the lowest branches of the trees surrounding us, their beady eyes focused on Aurora and their tongues drawing across their beaks.

Fury racing through me, I pushed Aurora and Acesca behind me and growled, ready to fight for my life if they tried to take Aurora from me while we headed back toward Hades's palace. Nobody was fucking taking her from me.

A harpy swooped down and landed on her claws a few feet from me. "We're here for Dawn."

Another growl ripped from my throat, and I stepped toward her, about to wrap my hands around her throat and snap her in half. "If you're working for Hella, you can get the fuck out of here before I let my warriors slaughter every last one of you."

The bird-woman held up her wings. "We mean no harm. We need her help."

"You took that wolf from me," Aurora said, stepping at my side.

I laid a hand over her stomach and gently nudged her back, but she didn't budge. I should've known that she wouldn't. Even in those memories I had of us in our past lives, she never once backed down from a fight.

"He's dying," she said, voice cracking and shoulders slumping forward. She doubled over on the ground and shook her head, tears in her beady eyes. "He's been my lover for years now. I didn't want you to hurt him."

"I don't think we should trust her, Kitten," I said through the mind link.

Something didn't feel right about this, yet I didn't know if it was my intuition or just my mind fucking with me. Being here, where Mars used to live—up until today, it seemed—I could feel his presence, could feel and understand that he didn't trust many here.

And I didn't want to trust many people either, including these bird things.

"Please," the harpy begged, glancing back at her flock. "Bring him out."

"Are you sure?" another asked her, looking warily at Aurora and the warriors behind me. "It could be dangerous."

"I'm sure. They can be trusted."

The harpies moved to the side and showed us the wolf that Aurora had attempted to heal yesterday. Aurora had done as much as she could, but she must've not healed him completely. The wolf looked worse off than he had.

Aurora sucked in a sharp breath and stepped closer to him, but the harpies blocked her path and surrounded him.

The first woman stood back up from her knees and locked her fingers together. "Please, tell me that you will heal him. If you can't, then we will have to seek help from someone from Hella's kingdom."

The others shook in fear. "We can't do that," one said.

"We will have to," she said.

Aurora cleared her throat. "I'll try to heal him as much as I can, but you'll have to trust me to touch him. I'm not going to hurt him, like Hella and Nyx have hurt him and you in the past. He's not just your lover; he is an old friend of mine. I promise you that I'll do everything in my power to save him."

CHAPTER 11

MARS

"This is the first time I have seen Hella retreat," Helios announced, standing inside his home in the underworld. His flaming horses were perched outside in the clearing, the flames reflecting off his eyes. "Even with the surprise attack that she planned on your home this morning, she has never done that before. How did she even find your home? I can still barely find it, and I've been there plenty of times."

Flora pursed her lips together from beside him, arms crossed over her chest, looking more pissed than I'd ever seen her. "Hella's wolves found him. He saved them and didn't tell any of us about it."

I growled, wishing she'd just drop her little crush that she had on me. "They came to my home this morning to tell me that Ares and Aurora have made it to the underworld with reinforcements, including other packs and warriors."

Helios and the other gods stopped. "You're kidding me. She's here?"

"She's here," I repeated, warmth erupting through my chest.

"*If* he was telling the truth," Flora said. "You know how Hella is."

Helios ran a hand through his hair and paced the living room. "It makes sense, then. Hella wasn't fighting us with every wolf that she had. If she planned that attack on Mars's home this morning, she must've been planning for other hellhounds to show up. Maybe Ares and Dawn found them and stopped them. Maybe that's why they retreated."

Flora clenched her jaw, shook her head, and stormed out of the house, slamming the door behind her. I let out a low sigh, my shoulders slumping forward, and clutched Aurora's picture harder in my grasp.

Thank the Moon Goddess that Flora is gone.

"This might mean that we have a chance," I said. "We can win this."

Helios smiled along with the other gods. "We must spread the word. If everyone knows that Dawn and Ares, the god of war, are alive and back in the underworld, then they will have something to fight for again. We can inspire a revolution. I'll fly around the underworld and tell everyone I see to prepare. This war is ending soon."

After everyone cleared out of his living room, I shut the door behind me and sat on his porch steps, staring out at the forest and wondering if I should even head back to my home. Hella had destroyed it during the attack. I had nothing to go back to there now.

And if I went back, then Hella would know where I was. It wasn't something I could risk.

So, I closed my eyes for a moment of peace, falling into a daydream or memory or something...

* * *

"C OME ON!" *a young girl shouted, showing me a mouthful of gums. Her pigtails bounced as she looked back at me and ran through the forest, darting around the trees and giggling. "Don't fall behind, Kairo! I'm going to beat you to the lake."*

"You're not going to beat me anywhere!" A boy whizzed by me, his dark brown hair flopping against his forehead and his short legs almost moving faster than his body. "Get back here! I'm going to be the alpha."

"Nuh-uh!" the girl shouted. "I am!"

I followed them through the forest and watched from the trees as the boy sprinted fast, captured the little girl by the pigtails, and tugged on them. The girl yelped in pain, turned around, and punched the boy square in the jaw.

"I told you not to pull my pigtails!" she shouted.

"Yeah, but they're cute," the boy said.

She scrunched her nose, lips pressed into a tight line, and then she pulled on a strand of his long hair. "You should put your hair in pigtails. It's too long and messy. It doesn't look good on you, but pigtails would look cute, Kairo."

Kairo crossed his arms. "My dad says that boys don't wear pigtails. I asked him."

"Yeah, but you're not any boy," she said. "You're an icky boy."

Kairo lunged at her again, his tiny arms coming around her body, playfully pushing and shoving and yanking her down into the few inches of water underneath their feet. She let out a little yip, her giggles drifting through the forest once more.

My lips curled into a small smile, just as something grabbed at my heart.

A tree branch broke to my left. I glanced over my shoulder to see Charolette with short blonde hair standing behind a tree and excitedly watching the girl jump around and play in the lake. Charolette smiled, a tear sliding down her cheek, and looked away.

She whirled around in my direction, furrowed her brows, and paused. After a second, she shook her head and walked right through me

—right through my fucking body—and continued back through the woods, as if she didn't even realize that I was there.

Turning quickly, I ran after her. "Charolette! Wait!"

Yet she must've not heard me because she continued to walk. I hurried after her, wondering where her wig was and how she looked so much more alive now. When I'd left Earth, her skin had been pale and dry, almost as if she was dying.

"Charolette!" I shouted.

She stopped for a moment and looked over her shoulder at me, her eyes scanning the woods. Again, she furrowed her brows, and I stood in front of her, waving my arms frantically to get her to see me. Instead of noticing, she twirled around and continued until she reached a house.

Vulcan and Venus sat on the porch, chatting quietly.

Charolette walked up the steps and smiled at them, bowing her head. "I know that I'm not supposed to be here, but I really appreciate being able to see her even if it is from afar."

"Of course, Alpha Charolette."

Alpha Charolette …

Is this the real world? Is this actually happening in real time? Did Ares leave the pack to her when he retreated to the underworld with Aurora and the rest of our warriors? If so, then that must mean…

"I wish I could be a bigger part of her life," Charolette said, another tear racing down her cheek. "I know that my brother would have loved her. She's just like her parents—powerful and always ready for a fight. She's going to be the strongest alpha this world has ever known."

CHAPTER 12

AURORA

*E*ven though I knew nothing about harpies, I took the broken wolf from their leader into my arms and fell to my knees. My power swelled within my body, a force so undeniably strong, one that I hadn't felt in a long time.

"Be careful, Kitten," Ares said, glancing down at my stomach. "Don't push yourself."

My body had been through hell and back these past couple days with the birth and loss of my daughter, but I needed to do this. I needed to push through to take back control of my life and prove to myself that I was powerful—that one day, I would be able to kill Medusa for kidnapping our baby.

I also needed to do this for us, so we could win this war.

After taking a deep breath, I closed my eyes and placed my hands on the nearly dead wolf. His pain, hurt, and agony shot through me, weaving into my veins and crushing my already-beaten soul. Nobody should have to endure this pain anymore from Hella.

Nobody should have to—

Suddenly, the world around me turned a darker shade of black. I snapped my eyes open but could only see darkness around me. The wolf in front of me was gone. My pack around me was gone. My Ares was gone.

My heart thumped against my rib cage.

"What's going on?" I screamed, flailing my arms around to find that wolf again, to find anything, to get my bearings or something. Where was I? Was this a dream? Were we still in the underworld? Had we ever even gone to the underworld?

A light sparked within the pit of darkness, and I sprinted toward it until the murkiness started to fade and a house appeared. Vulcan and Venus sat on two rocking chairs, chatting with who looked to be Charolette from behind.

"Of course, Alpha Charolette," Vulcan said.

"I wish I could be a bigger part of her life," Charolette said, a tear racing down her cheek. "I know that my brother would have loved her. She's just like her parents—powerful and always ready for a fight. She's going to be the strongest alpha this world has ever known."

Instead of running anymore, I stopped in my tracks and stared at her back. She must be talking about my daughter; that was the only person she could be talking about unless … since we had been gone, Charolette had found out that she had another brother—maybe another brother by Fenris. She had always been so obsessed with him.

Can it be?

Vulcan stood from his rocking chair and walked over to Charolette, resting a hand on her shoulder. "The world has changed a lot since they've been gone, but hopefully, what they're doing will make a difference. She's grown into an incredible woman."

"Ares and Aurora would be so proud," Charolette continued, wiping some more tears away from her eyes. "I'm so upset that things had to happen as they did. I don't know how many more years I can go on alone … without seeing Marcel. He would be happy to know that by some miracle, I've healed."

"She's healed," someone whispered beside me, happiness and disbelief in his voice.

I knew that voice.

I snapped my head in his direction and stared in shock at the man beside me, hiding in plain sight at the edge of the forest with scars all over his body and eyes so bright that they could blind me.

My wolf purred.

Mars.

Warmth spread throughout my chest, my mind reeling with excitement. Unable to stop myself, I stepped closer to him to grab his hand, but it seemed like I hadn't moved at all. In fact, the distance was growing between us.

"Mars!" I shouted, hoping to get his attention. "Mars!"

Mars glanced over at me, his eyes widening slightly. "Kitten."

The shadows surrounded us again. I extended my arm to touch him, even if it was just a small scrape of our fingers against each other, as he did the same. But in the last second before our fingers touched, the darkness consumed him.

"No!" I screamed, trying desperately to memorize every inch of his changing face.

There were new scars that I hadn't seen before and small lines around his eyes, as if what Hades had said was true—Mars had been down here a long time.

I blinked a few times, the world around me becoming clear again. Ares hovered above me, staring down at me with worry, panic, and anger in his eyes.

"I knew that her body couldn't take this." He seethed at someone behind him. "Help her. She should've never healed that wolf for you harpies …"

After blinking a couple more times, I looked over at Acesca, who touched my neck and searched for a pulse. "She's still breathing. Her heart rate is just ... a bit high right now. It's similar to when mates see each other for the first time."

I glanced over to see the wolf I had been healing slowly sitting up and opening his eyes. When I turned back to Ares, I lifted my fingers and glided them across his face. For a moment, his facial features softened, and I thought it was Mars. Ares grasped my hand in his firm and rough hand, bringing me back to reality.

Whatever these visions that I kept having were ... Mars was having the same ones.

Mars was here.

"Mars," I whispered, voice dry. "Mars is close. I saw him."

"What do you mean that you saw him?" Ares asked me, brows furrowed together. He glanced up and behind me at someone else. "Someone get her some water. Her cheeks are pale, her voice hoarse."

In a moment, the leader of the harpies flew up behind us and handed Ares a container of water that they must've carried around. I sat up, glancing around the forest to see if I could find Mars watching us.

But I came up with nothing.

After sipping down the water, I smiled at Ares. "I saw Mars in my vision. I saw him, Ares."

Ares tucked some hair away behind my ear. "He's not here, Kitten."

"But don't worry. We have hundreds of harpies that fly around the kingdoms. While we're in the sky above, we'll keep a lookout for Mars," the leader harpy said, gathering her wolf lover in her wings. "If we find him, you'll know within a few minutes of spotting. We'll get you back to him, just like you brought my lover back to me."

AURORA

*A*s we walked back to Hades's kingdom to turn in for the night, the forest around us became deathly quiet. I hadn't been able to stop thinking about seeing Mars in that vision—or whatever that was. Yet it made me smile, knowing that he was still here with me.

Even if it was just a part of him.

I inhaled sharply and stopped along with Ares, who scanned the forest cautiously. Branches snapped about fifty meters to the northeast. With the rest of the pack behind us, I closed my eyes and listened for more noise. There had to be an entire pack of creatures lurking in the night for us to find, yet they were slow and didn't seem *that* menacing.

Still, before I could stop him, Ares shifted into a wild beast on all fours, his claws digging into the dirt and his golden eyes glowing deep through the darkness. The tree leaves and branches almost hid the sky above, hanging close to the ground. Ares growled ferociously and stepped under the branches.

"Ares," I whispered through the mind link.

Where is he going? What is he doing?

More branches snapped, and leaves crunched. Whoever it was … it sounded like they were approaching us and that there were many of them, maybe fifty or more. Yet, still, not even with my wolf senses could I hear their breath or smell their scents.

"Be careful," I said again. *"It could be the hounds. Fenris maybe."*

He lowered into a fighting stance, as if he was about to leap out into the forest and kill the first monster that appeared in our vision. Tail shifting back and forth slightly and saliva dripping from his canines, he growled again.

When the first hound walked out from the darkness and into the slight light that flickered through between the trees, I froze. Whispers broke out among the warriors, yet nobody moved. They hadn't seen us yet.

"The hounds," I said, my voice barely above a whisper, eyes growing wide as more skeleton and half-eaten bodies emerged from the woods, walking in a straight path somewhere else. "They're here, but they look so … so broken, so weak."

Acesca moved closer to me. "Alpha Vulcan told our pack that you and Ares found Fenris doing some magic on a bunch of dead wolves—wolves that we'd all buried at some point or another. And that when he tried to raise the dead, he was unsuccessful for some wolves. Do you think that they are those wolves?"

I scanned the forest, looking from each undead to the next and trying desperately to remember if I had seen any of them before. But honestly, most looked like skeletons, not like normal hounds with flesh and fur.

"Should we attack them?" someone asked.

"Wait," I ordered. It would be stupid to pounce on a large group without knowing how many more walked alongside them, but we wouldn't let them go free. We needed to do something to stop Hella from growing her army of the dead. "Let's see how many there are."

More and more continued to walk out behind the initial group of hounds, their movements slower and their bodies frailer and smaller than the typical hounds that attacked us in the Sanguine Wilds.

Then, suddenly, the group dwindled down, the last few hounds scurrying behind them. And the man in charge of it all brought up the rear. Fenris walked behind the group of undead, beside a fleshless and brittle skeleton body.

Ares froze, his ears perking up and his golden eyes growing wide as he looked at Fenris's companion.

"*What is it?*" I asked him through the mind link.

He let out another ferocious growl. "*Mom.*"

CHAPTER 14

ARES

Mom was a hound.

I didn't recognize her. I couldn't see those bright eyes that always used to stare down at Mars and me with so much love, no matter how hurt we were on the inside. I couldn't see that smile she'd faked, even when Mars asked her if Fenris was hurting her after he raped her. I couldn't even see her skin.

But her scent was one that I would never forget. Even in death, it would haunt me.

Rage and agony shot through my body, a fiery vengeance forcing me to growl once more. I didn't give a fuck if these assholes saw us because this time, I wouldn't let Fenris live. I would kill him and take back control of Mom.

She didn't deserve this. She deserved life.

"*Ares,*" Aurora said through the mind link, her voice a mere whisper. "*Please don't attack them. We're not ready for another battle. There are far too many of them. I don't think we'll be able to—*"

But as much as my mate pleaded with me, I couldn't stop myself from barreling forward.

I loved her with my entire heart and would do anything to protect her, but Aurora hadn't watched her mother get raped. Aurora didn't experience the pain and sorrow that Mars did every fucking day because he hadn't done anything to stop it.

Once another growl ripped through my throat, the hounds finally looked over at us. Collectively, they let out a bellowing roar and ran toward us, almost as if they had been trained to rip any human apart.

Sprinting forward, I latched my canines into the first hound and ripped his skeleton body to pieces. Fenris and Hella would bring him back someday and sometime, but it would take time and energy. If we got rid of as many of them as we could now, then it would be harder for her.

Fenris growled from across the forest. I snapped my head in his direction, watching him shoo Mom behind him. She ran backward through the forest and into the darkness, disappearing from my view. But I wouldn't let Fenris escape with her.

Now, I would kill him for good and take his bones, so Hella couldn't rebuild him.

Our packs clashed against each other, my pack easily snapping and killing these undead creatures for a second time in the past few days. Hella's army might've been growing, but it was getting weaker by the day.

Every time we killed these hounds, they came back weaker. The more death, the easier it would be to stop Hella once and for all. If we needed to fight over and over and over to protect our daughter, we would.

Fenris ran through the crowd, right for me, as if he wanted revenge—or something much more sinister because I'd kill him in the human world. He was stronger than I'd originally thought and still had some consciousness left inside of him.

Most hounds didn't.

But I refused to let him kill any more people I cared about. This was the end for him.

I sunk my teeth into his throat, snapped the bones, and towered over his crumbling body. Each brittle bone fell to the ground into a pile at my feet, the stench of it making me gag. But I didn't stop tearing apart the little flesh that he had left.

Last time, I had torn his body in half. This time, I planned to keep him that way.

A skeleton. Fleshless with brittle bones. Dead.

After spitting the last of his flesh from my canines, I transformed back into my human and glanced over my shoulder to ensure that Aurora was all right. She stood across the field with piles of bones around her and tears in her eyes.

"Kitten, what's wrong? Did one of them hurt you?" I asked through the mind link.

I gathered Fenris's bones in my arms and held them to my chest, vowing to one day piece him back together to torture the fuck out of him with Mars. As calm and collected as he was, I was sure that Mars would love to torture him too.

"I hate the hounds, but these people ..." She paused, looked up at me and frowned. *"Most of these people were wolves we knew, my old packmates. They don't know what they're fighting for or why. Hella is using innocent lives."*

Suddenly, red, pink, and orange—the colors of dawn—erupted in her eyes, completely consuming her wolfish gold eyes and human blue eyes. Her irises glowed brightly along with the veins and arteries throughout her body.

I inhaled sharply at the vigor coming off her in waves, the strength undeniable. *"Kitten."*

"I hate it!" she screamed, the mere sound so powerful that the trees blew wildly above us and all the creatures—wolves and hounds alike—in the forest stopped fighting around us. "I hate it so much! I will kill her! I will take these hounds back."

The hounds, even the sickliest and frailest, showed no sign of aggression anymore, so much so that our wolves didn't look comfortable even facing them in battle. We weren't down here to kill aimlessly; we were here to defeat Hella.

But maybe we could do that in other ways.

One hound walked over to the bones at Aurora's feet, head hung low. She collapsed next to the pile of bones and curled her bony body around the pile, a slight whimper escaping her throat. Though she couldn't communicate with us, I could still feel the pain shooting through her. Maybe these hounds did have a bit of life left inside of them.

"If you want to destroy Hella with me, follow me," Aurora announced to the hounds, eyes still shining red, pink, and orange, her veins completely glowing through her human body. "We won't hurt or kill any more of you. We'll protect you."

A rumble erupted through the hounds, and then the ones still *alive*—if we could even classify them as that—bowed their heads in submission. Aurora took a deep breath, her shoulders slumping forward and a small smile crossing her face.

"We have an army," Aurora said through the mind link. *"An army that will win."*

CHAPTER 15

MARS

"*Mars!*" someone shouted to me. "*Mars!*"

I glanced over at Aurora, my eyes widening at my mate. "Kitten."

She extended her arm to touch me, even if it was just a small scrape of our fingers against each other, and I did the same. This might've just been a dream—one of the many that I'd had of her since I'd left—but I needed to feel her skin on mine again.

"No!" she screamed, our fingers not once touching.

Every dream I had of her ... I never got to touch her. If I did, my body and my fingers drifted right through her flesh. I was like a fucking ghost down here in the underworld. If I ever really saw her again, I didn't know if I would ever be able to touch her.

It was hell down here. Literal hell.

"Mars!" she said again, but her voice sounded different. It was fading away, out of my dream of her.

* * *

"HE ONCE WAS a feared god of war," someone sang softly, stroking the strings of a lyre.

I lifted my head from Helios's porch post and slowly blinked my eyes open to see the dark night sky and forest before me. Apollo, the god of many things, leaned against the opposite porch post, humming and singing to himself.

"But now, he's become the god of sleep, god of the night, sleeping through the darkest of times," Apollo continued, eyes closed, as if he was having a grand time with his little song that he must've been making up on the fly.

After shifting slightly, I leaned my back against the post and arched a brow at him. A chuckle escaped past my lips, my chest feeling light, especially after the dream of Aurora that I'd had only a few moments ago.

I still couldn't believe that I had seen her. It was almost as if … it was really her and not just a memory of my mate. She looked slightly different; her eyes so tired.

"You're awake," Apollo said, his tone humorous. "Finally."

"I barely closed my eyes."

"You've been out like a light for an hour since I found my way here." Apollo placed his lyre down on the porch stairs and sat beside me. "Why is it that every time I find you, you're always sleeping, Mars? Dreaming of your girl?"

My lips curled into a soft smile, warmth spreading throughout my chest. "Yes."

Apollo chuckled. "Well, no more dreaming!"

"I can dream of Aurora as much as I please," I said, closing my eyes again. "In fact, I plan to dream about her again. You're welcome to stay and watch, but I'll be off to dreamland now before another hundred years pass for me. She's the only thing getting me through this."

"The only thing?" Apollo said, crinkling something.

I opened one eye and glanced over at him. "The only thing."

He pulled out a sheet of paper from his pocket, the same kind he'd used to draw that image of Aurora for me years ago now. There looked to be another drawing sketched on the sheet, but I couldn't really make out what it was yet.

"What about her?" Apollo unwrinkled the paper and handed it to me.

"What's this?" I asked, the young child looking oddly familiar.

"Your daughter."

My heart stopped. I sucked in a sharp breath and grasped the drawing tighter, unable to believe that Apollo had drawn a picture of my daughter. "How did you get this? Where did you find this? How do you know what she looks like?"

"Dawn," he said. "She and Ares are residing with Hades for the time being."

Suddenly, I shot to my feet. "They're what?"

"They're in the underworld, staying with Hades until further notice."

Unable to stop myself, I ran forward toward the dark woods, hearing the hollering and growling of Hella's pack of hounds closer than they should've been. She was closing in on us, but I knew where Aurora was. I needed to go get her.

But Hades's kingdom was so far. I wouldn't make it with Hella between us.

Still…

"You can't." Apollo wrapped an arm around my shoulders and pulled me back before I could get even a few steps away from the porch. "I would love to bring you there, but Hella's armies have invaded the territory between here and there."

"I need to find her."

Once he let me go, he lifted his shirt to show me the deep gash wound underneath it. "I almost died on my way over to you, traveling alone, even with my magic. Those hounds are becoming rowdier by the day. More have traveled through there since."

"But it's only been an hour," I said. "We have to go back."

"We can't," Apollo said. "If you do, they will trap you, just as they trapped Helios years ago."

"It's true," Helios said, stepping out of his home and onto the porch steps. "I once came down to the underworld to find the love of my life, and Hella forced me into a trap. She will use your love for Dawn and my sister against you."

"I need to see her again," I whispered, staring down at the image of my daughter.

"If Hella traps you in her castle, you won't ever see Dawn," Apollo said.

"Unless she traps Dawn, too, and tortures her in front of you," Helios finished.

And while I wanted to run into that forest, right into Hella's armies, I wanted to see Aurora more. I stared at the image of our daughter. I especially wanted to meet this girl at some point too. I couldn't do that if Hella trapped me down here for as long as she'd trapped Helios.

I refused to be her plaything.

CHAPTER 16

"You've brought back an entire pack of hounds to my kingdom?" Hades asked me, staring out into the forest, where the hounds were gathered, not a single one of them aggressive anymore. He crossed his arms and rocked back on his heels. "You really did, didn't you?"

I teetered back and forth on my feet. "Can they stay for the night?"

After a couple moments of silence, he nodded. "Yes, but we need to talk."

Once I thanked him, I urged our pack to make the hounds as comfortable as they could be. Most of them were tendons and bones, but at least we could try to make their stay as welcoming as possible. I was sure Hella hadn't done anything like this.

"I'll be back," I said to Ares, standing on my toes to kiss his cheek. "Please, help them."

Ares eyed me as I disappeared into the castle with Hades. He led me up a set of stairs and on to a balcony that overlooked the forest and the hounds below us. I leaned against it and stared down at the creatures who had been granted a second life.

"Werewolves are taught that the only strength they should train is the physical," Hades started. "You are physical beasts by nature and will fight to the death before giving in to someone or something else. I've seen it over and over with the hounds."

"We are," I said, feeling a sense of pride rush through me.

"But you didn't save those hounds down there with your brute physical strength."

My body tensed, and I shook my head. "No, I didn't."

"One of the first things that you'll learn down here is that the greatest strength that one can have isn't physical," Hades continued, glancing over at me and smiling softly. "It might sound a bit *cliché*, as you humans call it, but the greatest strengths in the underworld are perseverance and kindness."

I giggled—straight-up giggled—because, well, I didn't think he was being serious. He couldn't be, right? There had been a centuries-long war where monsters fought physically with each other. It wasn't like they fought with their kindness.

"The reason we haven't won this war yet," he said, hands tightening around the railing, "is because they killed you. Your sister, the moon, might be the one who created the werewolves, but you're the only one who has ever been able to tame the hounds. You show kindness to the creatures who have only been shown darkness because..."

I swallowed hard and stared into the dark forest. "Because I've seen the darkness with my mother. I know what it feels like to believe you're nothing but a burden, like nobody wants you around, like you have no power at all."

"And that's why you were able to tame those hounds today, to turn them into creatures that don't loathe humans and regular werewolves for no reason at all. You're here because you are the only person who can change this war."

While I would never forgive my mother for what she had

done, Hades might've had a point.

"You've always thought that your mother was out to hurt you," Hades said. "And you can completely feel that way. I'm not going to say that you shouldn't. But … you've been through hell and back for a reason, Dawn. Your mothers—your real mother and the one you grew up with—have put you through trial after trial to train you for this."

My hands tightened into fists by my sides as I held back hot tears. "Trials, huh?"

"Throughout every obstacle, you've gotten stronger and kinder. You could've turned into an evil bitch like Hella or Nyx, but instead, you've become a goddess who heals the people she knows and doesn't know alike, even hounds."

While I wanted to refute every single thing coming out of his mouth, I couldn't because he was right. My family had shoved me down so many times, and I still wanted to help and love people who I didn't even know. I could've become a monster, just like Hella, but instead, I refused and led my life the way I knew was right.

"I still hate my mother," I whispered, thinking about the drawing of my baby that Apollo had done for me. I hoped that if he hadn't found Mars yet, he'd make it to him and show him the image of our daughter. "Both my mothers."

"Fair enough," Hades said, a deep and cold chuckle behind his words. He followed my gaze out into the dark forest that surrounded us. "I hate some of my family too. It must be a god and goddess thing. Or maybe it's just an everyone thing."

I glanced over at him, my lips curling into a small smile. I didn't know the first thing about him, had only really had a couple conversations with him so far since we'd been down here, but I felt like I could really relate to him.

A growl rumbled through the darkness behind me. Shivers traveled down my spine, my arm hairs standing up and my heart pounding against my chest. My wolf purred inside me, the sound of her possessive mate making her excited.

"What's going on?" Ares asked, stepping on to the balcony with us.

Hades glanced over at me and gently nudged my shoulder. "If you need anything, you know where to find me. I'll let those hounds stay here for as long as you decide to stay in my kingdom, but everything you need to win this war lies outside of here. One day, you'll have to take that leap of faith and leave."

"That day will be tomorrow," Ares said, gripping my waist and placing me behind him.

Something had been going on with him lately while we had been down here. He had become a bit more agitated with the smallest things, annoyed and angry at people and hounds for no reason at all.

"There is no rush," Hades said, glancing from him toward me.

Another growl escaped Ares's throat, and he shoved me further behind him. "Yes, there is."

"And what is it?" Hades challenged.

"You."

Hades let out another dark chuckle and then tilted his head, as if giving Ares the win in whatever kind of argument they were having right here and right now. Then, he nodded to both of us and excused himself from the balcony.

When Ares finally turned around, I smiled up at him. After my talk with Hades, I felt … different. A lightness drifted through me for the first time in a long time. We might've come down to the underworld to end this world for good, but up until now, I hadn't known how we would do it. Now, I did. Now … I knew that there really was a chance we'd come out alive and get back to Earth to see our daughter.

All those trials, all those heartbreaks, had made me stronger in some fucked up way.

"We're going to change the ways of the hounds," I whispered

to Ares, my arms snaking around his waist and my head resting against his taut and strong chest. "We're not going to kill them all. I'm going to love them."

CHAPTER 17

ARES

$\mathcal{I}$ lay in bed next to Aurora and stared up at the dark
ceiling, dragging my fingers across the wounds I'd
received from the battle with the hounds earlier. All the wounds
had completely healed, only leaving small scars, which would be
gone by morning. But all those scars, all those wounds, would
weigh heavily on my mind.

Not in a bad way, but in one that I would always remember.

"You're returning to Ares," Aurora said, snuggling closer to
me and grabbing my hand.

"What do you mean?"

"I mean, after Mars died, there was a time when you became
like him. You were gentler and more loving and didn't snap in a
moment's notice. It was almost as if you thought I needed him
more than I needed you."

My jaw tightened slightly because she was right. I had held
myself back from flipping out recently, had tried hard not to be

my true self because Aurora *did* need the soft love that Mars had always given her.

But now, we had learned that Mars was still alive, that he was in the underworld somewhere, and the only way we would find him would be to fight Hella and all the monsters she threw at us. The only way we would succeed was if the real me came back and thrived.

It wasn't only that. I felt stronger down here than I ever had in the Sanguine Wilds.

"I want to tell you that being down here is fucking with my head, but I feel like I'm growing into myself again, into the man I used to be, the god who used to rule down in these parts. I'm making decisions and fighting in a way that feels so natural."

Aurora lightly pressed her lips on my shoulder, her scent filling my nostrils and calming me. I wrapped my arm around her slim waist and pulled her closer to me, the feel of her body against mine making me the happiest damn alpha alive.

"Which is why we have to leave Hades's kingdom," I announced.

Though I didn't know exactly how Aurora or my pack would take this news, I knew that it had to be done. I didn't like Aurora being around Hades because he had a certain charm to him that seemed to smooth over *everyone.*

And Aurora was mine.

I didn't care how over-the-top jealous that made me seem. I could've been worse.

"We're leaving. Tomorrow morning when we awake."

"Where are we going?" Aurora asked, staring up at me with those big, sexy fucking eyes.

"Home."

"Home?" she asked, brows furrowed. "Our home isn't in the underworld."

"Our first home," I said, grabbing her hand and standing strong. "To the one we made before Hella killed us both. I've had visions and dreams of it these past few weeks, and something is calling me to go back."

I didn't know what it was, but I needed to head back to the place where it'd all started, where this war had begun, where Hella had raided my home and tried to take Aurora from me during our first life together. I planned to reclaim the land, to show Hella that we wouldn't back down.

No matter what.

CHAPTER 18

MARS

The next morning, I awoke with an enhanced motivation to find my mate, to find Aurora.

Last night had been the longest one of my entire life. I had nightmare after nightmare of Hella finding Aurora and taking her away from me again. She'd screamed so loudly in my dreams, the shrill sound making me wake up multiple times in a cold sweat.

I needed to find her. It wasn't just a want anymore. She was in the underworld, so close to where I was, and I wouldn't let her travel around here alone anymore. Ares might've been strong, but he didn't know the horrors that lay upon this world down below.

There were monsters far more dangerous than Hella and Nyx. Giants and centaurs and birds who wanted revenge lurked in every dark corner of this realm, just waiting to attack and sink their claws into one's flesh.

Deep down, I wanted to protect Aurora because I couldn't

protect her in our life. I couldn't protect her in our past lives either. I had seen nightmares and horrors of what had happened after I died in the Sanguine Wilds. I had let Aurora die.

This was my only chance, my only chance to really see her again.

Part of me hoped, wanted, *needed* Aurora to be down here for me. For years, I'd prayed to the Moon Goddess to see her again. I'd wanted her to come and find me. But at the same time, I wouldn't be able to live with myself if that were the case. She shouldn't be down here at all.

"We need to get to Hades's kingdom," I pleaded with Helios as he walked into his small living quarters.

He had offered for me to stay with him from now on since Hella had destroyed my hidden home, but I couldn't wait here anymore.

"I know you think it's stupid. Hell, *I know* that it's stupid. But I need to find her. I need to find my mate."

"Mars, do you know how dangerous it is?" Helios let out a long sigh, rubbing the lines on his forehead, and then stared out of his living room window with a pained expression. "But I know. I know what it feels like to have your mate torn away from you."

"She's your sister," I argued. "Hella might still be here, still in between us and her, but we can't let her divide us. We need to find Aurora, Ares, and my entire pack. We're only gonna be able to defeat them together. Not separately. Hella has far too many hounds on her side."

Helios stared at me for a long few moments. Then, finally, his eyes softened, and he nodded. "I know, Mars. I know we need to find her now. She's the strongest god and goddess of them all, and she doesn't even know her true potential yet. She has the ability to lead the hounds. Not just the wolves, but also the hounds. Hella's hounds."

"What?" I whispered, my heart racing inside my chest. I swallowed hard and stared at him, my eyes wavering just a bit. *Aurora has the ability to not only wield the Malavite Stone, but to also lead the hounds?* "How is that possible? How can she lead Hella's hounds? Hella raised them from the dead with her own power. How can Aurora take control of Hella's creation?"

"It's possible," Helios said. "I've seen it with my own two eyes. When she was alive years and years ago, she was best friends with the hounds. They followed her wherever she went. Every time I saw them together, I couldn't fathom it, but it's true. She is extraordinary, even for a divine being."

"If what you're telling me is true and we get Aurora close enough to hellhounds, will she be able to lead them? Is it possible for Aurora to take control of the hounds just by using her mind?"

Helios sighed again. "I believe so, but I'm not certain. We'll have to check it out and see."

"Then, let's go." I leaped up from the small couch. "Apollo left hours ago. The hounds between her and us have dwindled down. This is our only chance. You know that Hella isn't going to give up her position. She knows that she's in between us, driving us apart. We need to get to Aurora now. Do you know any way to Hades's kingdom without going through her?"

Helios frowned, and then he perked up and hurried over to one of his many desks in his house. After pulling open a drawer, he took out a map and laid it flat across one of the tables. Then, he traced it with his finger and finally found a point on it.

"I believe there's a secret passage. We would have to pass the hounds, so we could do so in secrecy. I could use my magic—at least, all the magic I have left. We can try to cloak ourselves while we walk around the hounds. But it's very risky. We could get caught. And if we get caught, we might not survive. It's a choice that we have to make together if we want to try to find Aurora again."

After weighing all the possibilities of what could happen, I nodded. "Let's do it, then. We have to do it. We have to get to her now."

Helios looked over at me and nodded. "Okay, let's do this. We're going to go find Aurora tonight. I'm going to get you back to see your mate."

CHAPTER 19

AURORA

With my hands around the black balcony railing, I stared out into Hades's kingdom the next morning. My mind was racing and reeling with thoughts about what could happen once we left this safe place. Every other time that we had ventured beyond these walls, we had been attacked or fought monsters.

What if that was all we would be doing these next few days, weeks, months … years?

While I needed to find Mars badly, we needed to end this war now. We couldn't wait much longer. And with my newfound power of being able to lead the hounds, I knew now was the right time to leave.

We needed this more than ever.

And … Ares was getting a bit more possessive than he usually was, especially when Hades was around because Hades had always had a certain kind of charm to him, one that seemed to come naturally.

"Are you ready, Kitten?" Ares asked from the doorway. "We're leaving soon. All of our warriors are ready and waiting down in the foyer."

"I'm nervous," I whispered, placing a hand over my stomach.

I thought back to our little girl at home, the little girl who Medusa had ripped away from me. I had seen only glimpses of her in my dreams, but I knew that she was doing okay. I just … I needed to see her as soon as possible.

But if we died after we left Hades's kingdom, I would never get to see her. Never.

"What if … what if Hella kills us again?" I asked Ares. "She's tried to kill me so many times, Ares. You don't understand. I'm so nervous. I want to see my baby. I don't want to … I don't want to be another woman she kills again. I want to see our baby's face, just one time. Just one fucking time, I want to see it."

Ares came over and wrapped his arms around my waist from behind. He rested his head on my shoulder and gently kissed my neck, his lips lingering on my skin. "I know it's scary," he said. "I'm fucking scared too. But you will see her. I'll make sure of it. I'll do whatever the fuck I need to do to get you back to the Sanguine Wilds to see her. Anything."

He'd said it like he meant it, and I knew he did. And I knew this meant he would do anything, even sacrifice himself for me. But I'd already lost Mars, and I refused to lose him too. We were in this together. We were in this to stop this war and find Mars.

By leaving this kingdom today, we would find him. We had to find him. He knew more about the underworld than we did. He had been fighting Hella for what seemed like over a hundred years now. And I wanted to save him from that misery. I didn't want him to go on any longer without seeing our girl, without seeing me, without being with Ares.

"Let's go," I said, my stomach turning. I didn't know if this was the right choice or not, but we needed to go now.

After taking his hand, I pulled him out of the bedroom,

through Hades's castle, and down the grand staircase, where our warriors were gathered in the foyer. Whispers and murmurs drifted through the crowd, the loud hum echoing through the empty castle. Hades stood at the foot of the staircase, watching us. When we reached the bottom, I gave him a small smile and thanked him for everything he had done for us so far.

"You're welcome to come here more often. I look forward to seeing you, and I'm glad that I met you." He smiled back at me and then shook Ares's hand. "You too, Ares. If there's anything I can do to help you out on your journey, to help you kill Hella and Nyx once and for all, please let me know. I want this war to end just as much as you do.

"So many of my warriors have died because of it. So many of my close friends have left this world for a bit or forever." He looked over at me with sadness in his eyes. "But … we will come out on top. We will defeat her. Thank you for everything that you're doing. And I know that you'll find Mars."

After thanking him once more, I stood at the top step of the staircase. I looked at our warriors and cleared my throat, commanding all the attention. Everyone looked over at me, including the one female friend I had made here so far, who smiled supportively at me.

She could never replace Charolette, but I didn't know if anyone could.

"We will leave Hades's kingdom today," I announced. "And when we do, we must be prepared to face the worst of the worst. We will defeat the hounds soon. Too many of our brothers and sisters, of our packmates, have died. This time, we will win."

CHAPTER 20

*A*s Hades had promised, the road to Tartarus—the place halfway between Hades's and Erebus's kingdoms, where Hella and Nyx supposedly resided—was filled with monsters and hounds. After defeating some minotaurs and other bird creatures, the hounds began attacking us from behind.

A hound sprinted toward me, his canines drawn and dripping with blood. I leaped out of the way, my hands curling around Aurora's waist and pulling her behind me. Aurora might've had all the strength in the world, but she was still mine. I would do whatever it took to protect her and keep her alive to see Mars again and our daughter.

The hound sank his claws into my thigh and his teeth into my abdomen, pulling out a huge chunk of my flesh. A loud roar escaped my throat, and I tossed him off of me with my sheer strength. Then, I kneed him in the snout and sent him flying backward into a tree. The tree snapped and smacked against the ground, hitting three more hounds in its wake.

All I wanted was for fucking Fenris to show his face. I wanted to kill him this time.

I need to kill him this time.

Him running away with my mother last night had proven that he was weaker than when he had been in the Sanguine Wilds. If he hadn't been, then he would've fought and killed me too, like he had done with Mars.

But the more hounds I fought, the more I couldn't find him among the beasts.

From across the battlefield, I spotted a woman with eyes so dark that they haunted my nightmares. Hella stood among the beasts, hurling her magic at my packmates and *trying* to kill them. Some magic struck Aurora's newfound friend, sending her down.

I clenched my jaw and growled harshly to capture her attention. As I lunged forward to slaughter more hounds and to kill her, my mind suddenly became fuzzy with memories or ... maybe events that were happening now in the Sanguine Wilds.

A YOUNG GIRL, at least six years old, flashed through my mind. She had long dark-brown hair that cascaded past her shoulders. Her eyes were as bright as Aurora's and filled with so many of dawn's colors. She lunged forward toward an enemy boy too, mirroring my movements.

Canines drawn, she raced toward the boy and tackled him to the ground. They somersaulted down a slight hill. When they reached the bottom, she pinned him to the ground, her hands around his wrists and her body straddling his waist.

"Finally," she said breathlessly, chest heaving up and down. "I won."

"ARES!" Aurora screamed out in the real world, but I couldn't seem to get myself to come out of the hazy memory of this girl.

No matter how hard I tried, no matter how many hounds

tried to pile on top of me, no matter how much blood poured out from my fur, the only thing I could see was that young girl.

The boy grinned at her. "Nuh-uh. I let you win."

It seemed like the girl didn't like the way he'd responded to her, so she picked up her knee and thrust it right into his thigh. The boy whimpered underneath her and clutched his thigh, shaking his head and submitting to her. She got off him.

When he did, her eyes grew even brighter. "I told you that I won."

"Alphas always win," the boy said, getting off the ground and dusting himself off. *"You're not an alpha. Only I am, and there can only be one alpha per pack."*

Little did he know, that wasn't true. Both Aurora and I were alphas.

"I can be an alpha too!" the girl said, crossing her arms over her chest. *"Legend says that the first female alpha happened only a few years ago. But it still happened. If you can be an alpha because you're a boy, then I can be an alpha because I'm a girl."* She tossed some hair over her shoulder. *"And besides, I am stronger than you."*

The boy furrowed his brows, trying to seem angry, but there was a small smile on his face and almost adoration in his eyes. "Whatever you say," he said. "If that's what you want to believe, you can believe that."

"Well, that's what I believe," she said, mirroring his same curious and excited look.

There was something between them, something that I couldn't quite put my finger on.

She and the boy stared at each other for a long time. And then, suddenly, the boy stepped forward toward the young girl and kissed her right on the lips. Rage rattled through my body at the mere sight of it. Something inside of me felt so protective. And that same something told me that this just wasn't any girl.

This girl in my vision was my daughter.

My daughter was getting older and growing taller, experiencing life and love, and neither Aurora nor I were there for her.

CHAPTER 21

MARS

*O*ur daughter was just like Ares.

I stared at her in amazement while my heart thumped against my rib cage. So powerful, so strong, so hardheaded and short-tempered, but filled with so much emotion. And who could forget that smile and those eyes that mirrored Aurora's?

"I can be an alpha too!" she said, crossing her arms over her chest. "Legend says that the first female alpha happened only a few years ago. But it still happened. If you can be an alpha because you're a boy, then I can be an alpha because I'm a girl." She tossed some hair over her shoulder. "And besides, I am stronger than you."

My lips curled into a smile, and I faintly heard someone call my name in the distance. I didn't know if our daughter even had any of my traits. All I had seen so far, in every vision, was a young girl who was becoming just like Ares and Aurora.

Nothing like me. Nothing yet.

After our daughter bickered back and forth with the boy for a couple more moments, the boy leaned forward and kissed her. She

80

stared at him with wide eyes, in complete shock, and then kissed him back.

I watched them curiously, knowing that I couldn't stop what was happening and knowing that if Ares saw what I was seeing, he would surely flip his lid. He was a protective bastard, but he was my other half. Someone I thought I would never be able to live without.

Our daughter grabbed the boy's hands in her smaller ones and squeezed them hard, a tiny giggle escaping her lips. After a second, he pulled away, and they stared at each other as if they didn't know what they had just done.

"Kairo, what ... what was that?" she whispered.

The boy widened his eyes and then shook his head. "I don't know. I just ... I wanted to kiss you."

"But kissing is only for adults, even your dad said it."

"Yeah, but ..." The boy looked down, his face reddening. "I don't know. But if kissing is just for grown-ups, then why did you kiss me back?"

Our daughter looked down at the ground, too, and shrugged her shoulders. "I don't know either, but we can't tell the adults. You know how they are about you becoming an alpha. The elders... will punish us."

I tightened my jaw. Punish them? Nobody will punish my daughter.

"The elders said that they will find a mate for me, but I don't want anyone else," Kairo said, grabbing her hands. "I like you a lot, like a lot, a lot. I don't want to be apart from you. I want to be best friends forever."

SOMEONE SLASHED their claws through my abdomen, yanking me out of my daydream. All I wanted was more information. *Why is my daughter going to be punished? Who is Kairo to her? Why do I keep having these visions?*

But hounds surrounded me from all directions. I growled back at them, the saliva dripping from my canines. Hella's hounds sprinted at Helios and me from all over the forest. We had made it about seventy-five percent of the way to Hades's kingdom to find Aurora before the hounds attacked us. As far as I could see, Hella wasn't among them this time.

But Fenris was.

He stood behind the rest of his warmongering beasts and commanded them. It was like he couldn't fight anymore, and if he could, he wouldn't win a battle against me. In the Sanguine Wilds, he might have killed me, but I wanted to kill him now. I wanted to end his reign. I refused to let him hurt anyone anymore.

I wanted him dead for good.

So, I barreled toward him.

The closer I seemed to get to him, the more hounds I fought and killed, the stronger I smelled Mom's scent. I didn't know where she was, but she had to be here. He had tried to raise her from the dead at some point in the Sanguine Wilds. If he had been successful, she would be here. Fighting among the hounds.

More hounds piled on top of me, trying to stop me from reaching Fenris, who moved slower today, but I continued to push forward because I needed to get to him. I wouldn't let him escape this time. At least, not alive.

After roaring and thrusting back all the hounds, I sprinted at Fenris and latched my teeth into his neck, pushing him down. Easily, he collapsed to the ground. For a brief moment, he struggled underneath me. But his struggle wasn't enough. I held him down as hounds clawed into my back. Blood pooled from my body, but I didn't stop.

I was doing this for Aurora. I was doing this for revenge. I was becoming just like Ares.

Heart racing against my chest, I pinned him to the ground and refused to move. Helios captured the attention from some hounds on top of me, so they turned around and sprinted at him instead.

Fenris said something in ancient Latin—something I couldn't quite understand completely. And almost as if the hounds understood him, instead of sprinting at Helios, they ran away. They disappeared through the thick brush and fog.

Fenris stopped struggling underneath me.

And while we might not have defeated the hounds, I didn't want to kill them all. If there was a chance that Aurora could heal them and bring them on to our side, then we wouldn't slaughter them all ruthlessly.

And besides, now, we had Fenris–the hound made of bones–as our prisoner.

CHAPTER 22

AURORA

*H*ella hurled ball of magic after ball of magic at Ares, who stood, unmoving, in a trance. Blood poured out of multiple wounds in his body, his eyes glazed over, like they usually were during mind-linking someone, but his mind link was cut off from me.

I stared in horror from across the battlefield with tears rushing down my cheeks, pushing and shoving and killing hounds who stood in my way. "Ares!" I screamed, hoping I could snap him out of this.

He needed to fight. He *always* fought. *What the hell is he doing now?*

Some wolves in our pack tried to protect him, but they were easily overtaken by the instant surplus of hounds flooding into the lands. We had come so far without getting attacked, and now, we were surrounded from all directions.

"Ares!" I screamed again, sinking my teeth into a hound's neck and killing him. An overwhelming sense of sorrow washed over me because deep down, I knew that I could be saving these creatures. But right now, I could think of nothing but saving my mate.

I'd fucking lost too many people close to me. I refused to lose him too.

Another ball of magic hit Ares in the abdomen and sent him flying. I rushed forward, not giving a fuck about the hounds attacking me anymore. My wolf was reeling inside of me, aching to be set free. She forced me forward, canines lengthening and talons extending.

Sinking my claws into the dirt, I transformed into my wolf and ran forward toward the scent of my mate. I made it about twenty feet before a piercing pain shot through my head, giving me vertigo. The world spun around me, and suddenly, I wasn't in the forest anymore.

I was in the same cell that Nyx had locked me in centuries ago.

Still, I forced my body forward and pushed the thought from my head. It wasn't real. Nyx was here somewhere, hiding in the trees, trying to get inside my head to weaken me, trying to put me down like she had years ago. She was probably controlling Ares too.

When I saw the forest around me again, I spotted Ares, encircled by hounds, his body hanging over a tree branch, thick blood dripping down onto the hounds' snouts. The monsters clawed at the tree bark, growling through saliva-covered canines.

I need to—another wave of vertigo—*get to*—the world changed around me again, my vision becoming sanguine and black. Nyx stood in front of me with talons so long that they surely could kill me. She lunged at me in my fucking head, swiping her claws through the air.

As long as I was in this vision, Nyx had control.

I had to get out of it. I needed to think straight and refuse to see what she wanted me to see. I needed to protect my mate, to protect Ares, Mars, and our baby back home. It didn't matter what she did with me after all this. My family would survive.

So, I pushed through again. The vision faded around me, just as Ares's body fell from the tree branch and landed on the growling hounds underneath him. I shoved my body through the monsters, around my own packmates to try to reach my mate. He still wasn't fighting back.

Nyx had her claws so deep in him that he couldn't get out.

"Ares!" I screamed.

But the hounds' bodies swallowed him whole. I couldn't even see any bit of him anymore. They were pushing past me, closing in on him as much as they could, not even attacking our packs anymore.

Vertigo rushed over me, but I ignored that fucking bitch.

"Ares!" I screamed, power rushing through me.

I had to use my power to get him back. I needed to summon it to defeat them, but I didn't even think it would be enough. We were on Hella and Nyx's turf, not back in the Sanguine Wilds.

I thrust my hands against the ground, and a wave of dirt extended, shaking the ground and making some of the hounds tumble over. But my power wasn't strong enough. The hounds were bundled together so tightly that I couldn't get to all of them.

So, I did it again.

And again.

And again.

More time passed between each wave, each underworld-quake. Hella and the hounds took that extended time to start to retreat with *my Ares* in their possession. Tears streamed down my flushed face. My stomach turned.

I had to push myself. They couldn't leave with him.

"Aurora, you should slow down," Acesca said from behind me. "You're going to deplete your energy."

"I need to save him!" I screamed, thrusting my hands against the ground once more, but the tremble wasn't as strong this time.

Acesca was right; I was depleting my energy. If I kept this up, then I wouldn't be able to save him at all.

I couldn't take on Nyx and Hella alone.

Suddenly, a swarm of harpies rushed through the trees and toward us from behind, carrying the wolf I'd saved a couple days ago. They placed him down next to me and settled behind him.

The leader of the harpies stepped closer. "We found Mars," she said. "He's heading toward Hades's kingdom to find you."

"This is not a good time," Acesca said, pushing away some hounds. "They've captured Ares."

The wolf I'd saved hurried over to me and placed his forehead against mine, giving me some of my energy back. *"You know that you can't win this fight against her alone,"* he said through a mind link. *"You need to focus on the wolves. Get them on your side. They're the ones who have Ares. Hella does not."*

After a couple moments, I nodded and stared at the hounds, summoning the little power that I had left inside me. I closed my eyes and thought back to the thousands of years that I'd loved the hounds—both god-created hounds and hellhounds. They trusted me. They loved me.

When I reopened my eyes, one hound from the pack stopped walking with the others and looked back at me, the haziness fading from his eyes. Then another. Then another. But it wasn't enough.

Yet I continued.

More hounds stopped moving forward, and then Hella's screams echoed through the air. "Forward! Faster!"

The hounds I hadn't reached—there had to be close to a hundred thousand of them—started sprinting away with my mate's body. I tried. I tried damn hard to stop them with my power. But I couldn't.

I stood to my feet to run after them, but I collapsed almost immediately.

They had taken everything from me. They had taken the only hope I had left.

CHAPTER 23

ARES

"*I* want my daddy," my daughter said, sitting at a lake with her toes in the water. The boy sat next to her. *"Alpha Fenris says that he is strong, but ... if he is so strong, then why hasn't he come back? Why hasn't he come and found me yet? Alpha Fenris won't even tell me his name."*

I HAD BEEN WATCHING my daughter and the boy play fight, kiss, and then talk for the past half hour at least. Something had been happening outside of my dream—I vaguely remembered it—but I couldn't seem to escape this reality.

TEARS STARTED FALLING from my daughter's face. "Do you think that they'll ever come back?"

The boy pulled her closer and rested her head on his shoulder. "I think so."

"Are you just saying that?" she asked, brows furrowed together.
"No," he said. "They'll come back. They love—"

BEFORE HE COULD FINISH his sentence, my vision was suddenly gone. For a few moments, I kept my eyes closed, desperately wanting to see my daughter again. I wanted to savor the moment and remember everything that I had seen, so I could tell Aurora.

She would fucking love it.

When I opened my eyes, I stared up at the gray sky that moved above me. My body felt like absolute shit, pain shooting up and down my spine to my aching limbs. I grunted and went to move my arms, but they were pinned down.

I glanced around me to see thousands of hounds, some carrying me on their backs to a grand castle that I had never seen before. My heart rate spiked, my breath hitching.

Aurora ... where is Aurora?

Memories started rushing through me. When I had gone off into that vision, we had been in the middle of a battle with Hella and the hounds.

Where the hell did the time go? Have we been defeated? Have they killed Aurora again?

Struggling harder, I tried to move, but royal-blue magic chains kept my body straight and still. "Where the fuck is Aurora?!" I screamed, attempting to use my power and strength to get out of this bind that Hella must've put me in.

I had no fucking idea where we were, but I needed to get out.

My daughter was waiting for me.

"Let me out, Hella!" I shouted, but the chains only tightened.

"Oh, sweetheart," Hella said, abruptly appearing at my side with a menacing smirk and eyes that could kill. "You called me?"

"You fucking bitch," I said between gritted teeth, my hands balling into fists and my muscles tightening. "Don't fucking call me that. I have never and will never be yours. What the fuck did you do to Aurora?"

"Why do you need to bring her into this?" Hella asked, shaking her head and looking toward the castle. "Forget about her. She's done nothing for you, only held you back with power. This is your new home, and I'm your new Aurora."

"You're fucking insane," I shouted, struggling more. "Let me out!"

"No can do, sweetheart." She looked down at me and drew her tongue across her fanged teeth. "And don't try getting out. You won't make it past my magic. I've been studying you and your power for thousands of years. I know how to stop you."

"I'll kill you," I said.

"Good luck," she said, brushing her cold fingers across my bottom lip. Then, she turned away and cleared her throat. "Bring him to my chambers and lock him in the dog cage I set aside for him. He's going to be my puppy until he learns that I'm his alpha now."

While Hella disappeared into the swarm of hounds, some of the hounds broke off and started walking toward the entrance of the castle. I wanted to struggle more and more, but I knew that I would never make it out like this.

I needed to reserve my energy, so I could formulate an escape plan.

They carried me up a set of stairs and then into the dark castle. I looked around, taking in as much of the castle and trying to remember every inch of it. I needed to fucking memorize this shit if I wanted to get the hell out of here.

After walking me up a flight of stairs, we passed an office. Just as we passed, a man with white hair looked up at me, his eyes widening. I snapped my mouth shut, my heart pounding inside my chest.

Marcel.

Time seemed to slow down. He placed his book down on the

desk in front of him and watched as we moved past the doorway and toward the bedroom at the end of the hall. I stared back for as long as I could, knowing that I had a way out.

Or at least, I hoped I did.

Who knew what they had done to Marcel while he had been here?

CHAPTER 24

MARS

We needed a place to lock up Fenris, and the only place I could think of was Hades's kingdom. That was where we were headed anyway, and hopefully, we would be able to get there before Aurora left. I wanted to see her so badly that it hurt me, physically and emotionally.

If we got there and she wasn't there, I didn't know what I would do.

I grabbed on to Fenris by the scruff of the neck, my claws digging into his flesh and a rage burning inside of me—rage that only Ares felt. I knew that he was down here; I could feel his presence. Only he would leave behind such a strong aura of hatred.

The forest was littered with monsters, both dead and gravely wounded. I could faintly smell the scent of my pack, of Ares, and of my Aurora. They were close. So close.

"His kingdom is right up here," Helios said, glancing around the eerily quiet forest. We had been here a hundred thousand times, it seemed, yet something felt off today. It almost seemed harder to find. "It has to be, but this fog … it's almost too much."

I squinted my eyes and stared into the foggy forest. When we were in the Sanguine Wilds, the fog only came when the hounds were around. If the hounds were here, then that meant that my pack was probably out here, fighting them, killing them, and hopefully not dying in their sharp, bloody teeth.

"Let's keep moving," I said, tightening my hold on Fenris. "I'm not going to stop until we get there. We need to lock him in a cage and then torture the fuck out of him." Rage burned within me. I knew that this really wasn't me talking, but Ares. Or … maybe it was me. Maybe this place and seeing Hella day in and day out had made me hate everything.

The farther we walked into Hades's kingdom, the more guards patrolled the area, walking back and forth, as if they were on the lookout for something. Everyone seemed a lot tenser this morning than the last time I had seen Hades.

And then the grand castle came into view, the tips of it scraping the clouds. I stopped in awe, the way I always did, and stared at the palace. Something deep inside me stirred—a feeling that this was something I'd always desired. I wanted to be able to have a castle, a community, and a pack again with Aurora. It was what I'd wanted for hundreds of years, maybe even before I died the first time.

After a few moments of taking it all in, I picked up Fenris in one of my hands and stormed toward the castle steps. A couple of guards blocked me from hurrying up, as Hades didn't enjoy many unwanted visitors, but then he walked out the double doors and descended the steps.

He looked at me in confusion at first, brows furrowed and eyes wide, and then his gaze dropped to Fenris's body dangling from my hand, his blood dripping onto the carefully crafted stone underneath my feet.

"You … you captured him," Hades said, nodding to three

guards, who tried to take Fenris from me, but I refused to let this man go. Not after everything he had done to me, not after he'd brought Mom back to life.

I would deal with him now—and forever—until I killed him for good.

"Where is your prison?" I asked.

Once Hades nodded toward a door in his castle that led underground, I stormed toward it, with Helios close behind me and Hades on his heels.

"Nobody has ever been able to capture Fenris. How did you do it, especially with Hella and Nyx fighting alongside him?"

"Hella and Nyx?" I asked, yanking open a cell door and locking chains around Fenris's throat, wrists, and ankles. I didn't know if these chains would be strong enough, so I took another set of them and wrapped them around his entire body, ensuring he couldn't move even an inch. "Hella and Nyx weren't with Fenris when we fought him."

"No?" Hades said, turning away and pacing the prison floor. "But … there's been nothing but howling outside my borders for the past hour."

"That wasn't us," Helios said to Hades.

Hades's face paled. "Then, it must've been Ares and Aurora."

My entire body froze and then tensed. "Ares and Aurora? They're not here?"

"No, they left an hour ago to head toward Hella and Nyx's kingdom. I thought for sure you would've seen them. Their entire pack and even some of my guards left with them. Ares was dead set on leaving this morning."

I had known that I smelled something. I had known that I smelled them.

My heart shattered into a million fucking pieces. I had been so close, so fucking close to finding them finally. I'd been down here for ages, a century almost, looking for my mate and my other half. And I had missed them by one hour.

One. Fucking. Hour.

I balled my hands into fists and wanted to do nothing but hurl them at Fenris over and over. This was his fault. This was Hella's fault. This was Nyx's fault. If they hadn't wanted to kill Aurora, we would not even be down here. If Hella wasn't a crazy fucking bitch and wanted me more than anything, then we would be with our baby.

I needed to find them. I needed to find them now. They couldn't have gone far.

"I didn't hear any howling," I said. "Do you think that they … got attacked by Hella on the way over to her kingdom? Do you think Ares and Aurora killed them? I know Hella would never kill Ares, not down here, where deaths are final."

If it were the other way around and they touched Aurora, then Ares wouldn't stop howling and fighting and killing man after man, woman after woman for revenge, for hatred, for her.

"I don't know," Hades said, ascending the stairs toward the main staircase that led back outside into the foggy forest.

It had cleared up only a smidgen since we had been out here a few moments ago, which meant that the hounds were leaving this place.

My stomach turned. Was that a good thing? I didn't know.

Hades leaned over a railing, lifted his arm toward the northwest, and pointed. "They went that way only an hour ago," he said. "Once I started hearing the sounds of war, I sent guards to find them, but nobody has come back. I knew that they should've stayed here a bit longer. I knew that Hella and Nyx would be out today, but Ares was so stubborn."

"I have to go," I said.

There wasn't any way that I would let Ares and Aurora face Hella alone.

"Wait for me," Hades said. "I'm tired of sitting around and protecting this castle for nothing. Everyone who passes through here either doesn't come back or comes back gravely wounded. I refuse to sit back anymore. I need to make a call to some other gods, and then I will accompany y—"

Suddenly, he stopped and lifted his gaze to the western border of his kingdom. I followed his glance and sniffed the air rolling in from that direction twice. It smelled like … just like …

A young woman walked out from the forest with a pack behind her, and in her arms was my mate, my Aurora. In that moment, time—which happened so much quicker for a ghostlike entity like me—seemed to stop completely.

My mate was here.

CHAPTER 25

AURORA

At some point while I'd run after Hella's retreating figure, my body had collapsed. I could barely move. I'd pushed my wolf and my power far beyond its limits, more than I should've. More than Ares would've wanted me to.

Acesca carried me in her arms, instructing the others to follow her. I didn't know how many of my packmates had died during that little battle with the hounds and Hella, but it had been quite a few because I hadn't been thinking straight. All I could think about was saving Ares.

And I couldn't even do that.

Suddenly, the wolf inside me, who couldn't move and had been cursing me out for the last half hour because our body wasn't strong enough for our power, stirred restlessly inside me. I shifted in Acesca's arms, and she stopped.

Everyone around us stopped too.

"Oh my gosh," she whispered, and the pack erupted into a sea of murmurs.

"What is it?" I asked, blinking my eyes open.

After scanning the woods, I glanced up at Hades's castle standing before us. She must've led us all back here, so we could regroup and stay safe. But still, I didn't think that she would stop just because of—

Mate.

Mars stood at the foot of the stairs and drifted toward me quickly, his feet barely touching the ground and his body almost ghostlike. Almost. My wolf forced me to scramble out of Acesca's arms and stand on our own two feet.

Mate! Mate! Mate!

The first few steps that I took toward him, I stumbled. My knees gave out for a brief moment. But I pushed myself up and continued, slowly regaining my strength.

Mars ran toward me, and I sprinted forward. Wanting to touch him. Needing to hold him. Desperate for him again. I had been starving without him for the past few weeks. It had to have been worse for him—I could only imagine not being with anyone.

When he reached me, he scooped me up into his arms and held me tightly to his chest. I wrapped my legs around his torso and my arms around his shoulders, and then I buried my face into his neck and cried. Hard.

"I missed you," I whimpered. "I missed you so much. So fucking much, Mars."

Mars held me like he hadn't seen me for centuries, like he hadn't been touched in so long, so fucking long. So many emotions were rushing through my head, but I couldn't stop touching his ghostlike body as much as I could.

His body wasn't the same Mars that I had loved, but I didn't love him any less for what he had become down here in the underworld. He had lived and died for me, for Ares, and for our little girl. He had sacrificed himself for us.

"I'm sorry that I'm not the same," he said, his first words to me. "I'm sorry that I'm not the old me. I know it's different. Some parts of my body can float right through objects. My body isn't solid the way it was. I think it's because Ares is still out here, the other half of me. I'm sor—"

Before he could continue, I pulled his face closer to mine and kissed him hard on the mouth. It didn't matter to me at all. All that I cared about was that I could finally see him again, that I now had hope we could all be one happy family again one day.

"Don't explain yourself," I whispered, curling my fingers into his hair. "You're perfect. You've always been perfect to me." My words drifted off, the pain I held in my heart from being away from him slowly fading away.

"Where's Ares?"

My entire body froze, the tension spreading throughout my body again. This was bound to come up, yet I didn't know how to tell him that he had missed Ares by mere moments, less than a fucking hour.

"Aurora?" he asked, pushing some hair from my face. "Where is he?"

"Hella captured him." My chest tightened, and tears pricked the corners of my eyes. "I'm sorry. I couldn't protect him. I tried to get him back, but Hella and Nyx's powers together are too much for me alone. Nyx put him in a trance that he couldn't escape."

Something crossed Mars's face, wondering, awe, maybe sorrow.

"He is so strong," I said, lips quivering. "I'm not sure what he saw in that vision, but it must have been something serious if he couldn't snap out of it. It was as if it was more important than the war we were fighting. I don't know what—"

"Our daughter," Mars suddenly said.

"What?" I whispered.

"He saw our daughter," he said.

"How do you know?"

"Because I've been seeing visions of her growing up," he said. "We're still connected."

My heart broke even more. "Growing up?" She was growing up without her mother and father, without a family that loved her, with a pack that was probably still trying to survive in the Sanguine Wilds.

"But if he's with Hella now ..." Mars said, trailing off. "We need to get him back."

ARES

$\mathcal{I}$ could barely move.

Every single time I tried to escape this dog cage that Hella's servant had placed me into, every time I touched the silver bars that bound me here, my skin would sizzle. This silver metal was stronger than anything in the Sanguine Wilds.

The door opened, and I held my breath at the thought of seeing Hella. I wanted to rip her to shreds for what she had done to me. I only hoped that she hadn't laid a finger on my Aurora because if she did…

My chest tightened, my throat closing up. If she touched Aurora, I would lose it.

Instead of Hella—or Nyx—Marcel walked into the room. I sucked in a deep breath, watching his every single move, yet still, he didn't look over at me. Not one fucking time. He was either ignoring me or they had done something to him.

Something that I wasn't sure I wanted to know about.

"Marcel," I whispered, glancing over at the door to make sure that Hella wasn't following him into the room. I stopped struggling to conserve my energy, let one wolfish ear listen for when Hella was nearby, and then focused all my attention on Marcel. "Marcel!"

He didn't even acknowledge me.

"Please, look at me," I pleaded, wanting to get us both out of here as soon as possible.

He didn't look healthy or alive down here with Hella. If Charolette saw him …

"What have they done to you? I know you're in there. I know you can hear me."

Still, he didn't say a word. Instead, he walked over to Hella's bedside and pulled down her comforter, and then he drew her curtains closed, so her room was darker. He walked around the room, fixing up other smaller things, almost as if he was preparing for her to arrive.

"We don't have much time. She's coming," I said, glancing over at the door and hearing footsteps. Deep down, I knew that Marcel wasn't listening to me, maybe he wasn't even hearing me either. I needed to get his attention now, so I used my alpha tone. "Get me out of here now."

Nothing.

Absolutely nothing.

I stared at him in both horror and disgust. Hella and Nyx must've done horrid things to him—things that they would do to me and the rest of my pack if they found them. I couldn't let that happen. I needed to do something. Anything.

"You saved my sister," I said in a last-ditch effort. "You saved Charolette."

Marcel paused, his body going rigid. For the first time tonight, he was really listening to me because this involved his mate. He was down here for her, not for getting me out of these chains that I'd found myself trapped in.

"Charolette," I repeated. "I've seen her in my dreams. She's alive and healthy."

He stood up taller, his body still tense but his gaze now focused hard on the floor, as if he was trying to ignore me but physically couldn't. Thank the Moon Goddess for a mate bond. I wouldn't have been able to get to him in any other way.

"Say her name." I moved to the edge of the dog cage and grasped the silver bars, ignoring the searing pain shooting through my hands. "Say her name, Marcel. I know that you remember her. She's your mate. Say it once."

More footsteps moved down the hallway toward this room. I pleaded with him. *I*, Ares, the fucking monster, pleaded with Marcel to remember the woman he would do anything for, the woman he'd died for to protect.

When he still didn't say anything, I decided to turn it up a notch.

"If Charolette saw you now, she would be disgusted."

A feral growl escaped his lips, and he turned around to bare his canines at me. It'd worked. He had awoken a suppressed beast, an animal locked in a cage for far too long. Marcel had become a ghostlike entity like everyone had said Mars had become, which probably meant that time was flying by so much quicker for Marcel.

He could've been down here for what felt like hundreds of years, too, without his mate.

But one single word, one name, had changed it all.

Marcel still remembered her. There was hope.

Suddenly, Hella walked into the room, shut the door behind her, and locked us inside with her. I growled at her, my nails lengthening into sharp claws that ached to slash her throat and end this all.

"What did you say to get him all riled up?" she asked Marcel, unbuttoning her shirt.

Marcel didn't say anything.

Has he lost his voice? Has it been taken from him?

"Let me the fuck out of here, Hella," I growled at her, rattling the cage. Skin melted and dripped off the palms of my hands, and I pulled my hands away and bit back a whimper. I couldn't fucking let her see me weak.

I needed to find a way out of here, and this wasn't it. I would never break these chains, never mind the chains and the bars of the dog cage.

Hella continued to pull off her clothes until she stood naked in front of Marcel and me. I forced myself to look away, but she was using her magic to drive my gaze to be on her and nobody else. And this silver had already weakened me.

She crawled up onto the bed and lay back flat, spreading her legs and curling her finger at Marcel. "Come up here, Marcel," she said. "Teach Ares what he's going to be doing very soon. Teach him how to please me."

Marcel tore his guilty gaze away from me, his entire body still tense and his jaw still twitching. If he hadn't been in my pack, I wouldn't have been able to tell how he was feeling. But we were still so close despite not seeing each other for what felt like a long fucking time.

He was hurting.

He didn't want to do this.

Yet he crawled up onto the bed and dipped his head between Hella's legs to eat her out. I wanted to look away so badly. I didn't want to watch this or feel his pain. He still loved my sister but— like I couldn't look away because of Hella's magic—he couldn't stop himself from doing exactly what she asked.

"Good boy," Hella cooed, grasping his silver hair and holding his head down against her cunt.

I was torn. Completely and utterly torn. My brotherly instincts wanted to tear Marcel apart, too, but my alpha instincts told me that he didn't want to do this. He'd really rather never live another day in this world than do this with Hella.

But he was a slave.

Hella would do what she wanted with us. We were *both* her slaves now.

CHAPTER 27

MARS

I walked alongside Hades and Helios with Aurora in my arms toward Hella's kingdom. She shifted and stared up at me, tucking away some dark hair behind my ear. It had grown out far too long since I'd been down here, but I didn't have anyone to cut it. Hell, I hadn't been taking care of myself at all without her, because my only goal all this time was to see her again.

After running her hands through my overgrown scruff, she sighed softly. "I can walk on my own. You don't have to hold me. I can be strong. I've had to be strong for the past few weeks without you."

"If what Acesca said is true and you nearly just passed out fighting Hella, I'm not letting you walk around here. You need to get healthier and get your strength back because if Hella comes over here and tries to fight us again, she might kill you."

My chest tightened. There was no way in hell that I would let that happen. Hella wouldn't take somebody else away from me.

She already had Ares. And I hoped to fucking God that Ares would make it out of there alive. I didn't know what went on in Hella's kingdom. I'd made sure to stay away for as long as I could.

But I couldn't stay away any longer.

Aurora wrapped her arms around my shoulders and rested her head on my chest, staring up at me with her big blue eyes, full of wonder and happiness. But there was something else in them —something dark that I hadn't really seen before.

She'd lost everything—from me, to Ares, to our daughter, to a family and pack.

"It's getting dark," Hades said. "We should stop soon."

"Yes," Helios said. "If we don't stop, the monsters will come out and attack us on our trek to Hella's kingdom. We need to find a place to hide, to sleep. I'm not sure if all monsters will attack us, especially with Hades being here, but still, the hounds will."

"Okay," I said, nodding up the path we'd been walking to the nearest mountain. "I know a place up here, a cave within the mountainside. We can stop there for tonight, and hopefully, everyone will have healed completely by the morning."

"Stop for tonight?" Aurora asked, worry etched into every inch of her face. "Will Ares survive? I wanted to find him tonight. I don't want him to be there a second more than he should. What if he's still in that dream state? Will he ever come out of it?"

"Dream state?" Helios asked.

"Nyx put Ares into a dream state during our fight," Aurora said. "She had put me into one during a hound fight in the Sanguine Wilds while I was pregnant. She can … control the mind and the things we see."

Sadness washed over Helios's face, and he stared at the ground. "Maybe that's how she made me fall in love with her hundreds of years ago. Maybe she put me in a trance for however long we were together, pretending to be someone she wasn't."

Everyone went silent. It wasn't a secret. We all knew that Helios was one of the reasons that this war had started. He'd loved Nyx, and Nyx was jealous of the affection he showed his sister, Dawn or Aurora. So, Nyx killed Aurora and promised Helios she had nothing to do with it.

But Helios had been broken all those years ago without his sister.

He stayed silent, and then he reached over and gently squeezed Aurora's shoulder. "I don't know if I've told you since I saw you last, but I'm so fucking glad that you're back. I will never forgive myself for not seeing who Nyx truly was years before she killed you."

Aurora frowned and shifted in my arms again, wanting me to let her down, but I refused.

"It's okay," she said, though I wasn't sure if she remembered everything that had happened in her first life. She'd told me that she had visions of what our life was like before we both died and came back to life, but it had been blurry to her. "I just want to know if Ares will come out of the trance eventually. When Nyx trapped me, it was only for a couple moments."

"Ares couldn't even feel anything in the dream state," Acesca—who I'd learned was one of Aurora's friends and an amazing healer—said. She handed Aurora some herbs from a package. "Eat these. You're still looking a bit pale from earlier."

After Aurora ate the herbs, she turned to us. "Do you guys know if Ares will survive?"

We approached the mountainside and started up it, heading toward the cave.

Hades glanced at Helios and then at me. "I don't know much about her power," Hades said. "But she was strong enough to kill a god and goddess. If she can do that, then I assume she's strong enough to … keep Ares like that for a long time."

Aurora stiffened in my arms, shoved her face back against my chest, and stayed quiet. I could feel her body on the verge of crying, but surprisingly, she held herself together and just whimpered softly to herself. "I want to see him again. I don't want him to be brain dead."

"He won't be," I said, leading my pack into the cave. "We'll find him beforehand."

Though I wasn't sure if we really would.

Hella and Nyx together were some of the strongest gods in the underworld. We might've had Fenris behind us, locked in thick god-resistant silver chains, being dragged along by the chain around his neck. He lay almost lifelessly on the ground with tape around his eyes and nose, deprived of as many senses as possible. But he was only part of the problem.

We needed to separate Nyx and Hella to weaken them.

Someway. Somehow.

"Let's regroup in the morning," I announced to my packmates, who had been pleased to see me again. "Rest up and heal as much as you can. Hella's kingdom is only half a day's walk away by foot from here."

Once everyone started preparing to sleep, I brought Aurora to the very back of the cave and sat down with my back against the wall and her still in my arms. Now that I had Aurora, I didn't plan to let her go.

"I'm so afraid for Ares, but … I love being back in your arms," she whispered.

"I love that you're here, Kitten," I said, admiring her and her strength.

This woman had birthed my child and then given her up to fight for our freedom. Not many people could do that to ensure a better future for their offspring and their people. Only a true leader and alpha could.

"Kitten," she repeated, her voice soft. "I missed hearing that nickname roll off your lips."

A low chuckle escaped my lips because I had missed calling her that too. This felt so surreal—that she was down here in the underworld with me. I almost thought that *this* was a hallucination from Nyx.

"You look exactly the same too," she said.

"How did you expect me to look?"

"I'm not sure," she said, gently shrugging. "It's kinda crazy that there are two of you who look exactly the same in the underworld."

After a few moments of silence, her smile turned into a frown. "I'm sorry that I couldn't stay with our daughter. You don't know how hard it was for me to leave her. She was ripped right from my body, and I ..." Tears welled up in her eyes. "I miss her so much. I don't even know what she looks like."

I reached into my pocket and pulled out the drawing that Apollo had given me, and then I set it in her hands. "Why don't you take this back to start?" I said, wrapping her slender fingers around the edge of the picture. "This is our daughter, Kitten, and no matter what happens, I'll make sure she knows that you love her."

A tear slipped down her cheek. "Thank you, Mars," she whispered, body tensing. "Thank you so much."

AURORA

"Kairo, when do you think we'll shift into our wolves?" my daughter said to a boy.

Unlike last time, when I had been able to see her face clearly, this time, it looked fuzzy, almost as how I imagined what the world would be like for someone who needed to wear glasses. But I did notice how soft her dress looked, the dawn colors drifting in the wind.

She and Kairo stood behind some trees and watched the wolves run in the early morning, their fur blowing as they propelled themselves forward, their snouts pointed to the fading moon in the sky, and the scent of the Sanguine Wilds floating heavily through the air.

Goddess, I miss this. I wish that I can be here with her, whoever she has become since I have been gone.

"I'm not sure," Kairo said. "Dad said maybe when we turn thirteen, but no young wolves have shifted since those people departed into the underworld. At least, that's what he told me last night."

"Really?" my daughter asked, eyes wide.

"Yeah," Kairo said, stuffing his hands into his pockets and staring at *the older wolves running through the Sanguine Wilds. "My dad says that I'll need to start training with them," he said to her, leaning back against the tree and sliding to the ground. He kicked around some dirt with his bare feet and broke a twig in his small fist. "He said I won't be able to go out on adventures with you much anymore."*

My daughter crouched in front of him. "What?" she whispered, voice barely audible.

"He said that I need to prepare to become alpha and that the elders said that they will pick a mate for me in a few years, so I need to be strong for her." He stared at his feet, not glancing up at my daughter once. "The gods and goddesses who left the Sanguine Wilds haven't come back. Choosing two powerful mates is our best chance at survival."

"But, Kairo," she said, voice cracking, "we are supposed to be together."

As I stood behind a tree and watched them, my heart ached. All I wanted to do was run over to her and scoop her into my arms. They might have been mates, they might've not, but this was rejection. And rejection fucking hurt.

"We can't," Kairo said. "Dad said that today is the last morning I can spend with you."

"Kairo, no," my daughter said, dropping to her bum next to him, wrapping her arms around one of his, and then resting her head on his shoulder. "Please, don't let him take you away from me. We stay out every morning."

"He's the alpha. I have to do what he says."

"First, it will be mornings. Then, it will be nights. Then ... I will never see you."

Kairo stayed quiet, and I bit back some tears. I had already missed so much of her life. I didn't know when I would ever get to see her or if I would ever see her again. I just wanted to hold her and tell her that what was meant to be would be. Eventually.

Nothing came easy in the Sanguine Wilds. Not for our family.

"Aurora!" someone called.

And for a moment, I thought it was my daughter. Both she and

Kairo were looking in my direction and stopped talking, stopped moving, stopped ... breathing.

"Aurora!"

I blinked my eyes open, my dream suddenly gone and so very far away from me. If I could stay in that dream state forever, then I would. I wanted to be with my daughter so badly, wanted to smell her scent and be there when she shifted for the first time.

"You slept in late, Kitten," Mars said, sitting behind me with his strong arms wrapped around my torso and his fingers gently rubbing circles around my skin. "You seem like you slept well. I've been trying to wake you up for the past half hour."

I rolled onto my stomach, lying flat on the cave floor, and stared up at him. "I dreamed of our daughter. I didn't want it to end. She's getting so much older. I want to be there with her. We're missing a huge chunk of her life."

Mars suddenly went quiet and nodded. "I know."

"Do you think we'll ever be back to see her?"

Instead of reassuring me like he always did, he shoved his hands underneath my armpits, pulled me up, and sat me on his lap. Then, he brushed a few strands of hair off my forehead and behind my ear. "I hope so."

After running my hands through his messy hair, I frowned. "Me too."

We sat in silence for a few moments, listening to the early morning sounds of the underworld. People were gathered outside the cave, more gods and goddesses glancing in and smiling at me, as if they remembered me. But I didn't know who the hell they were.

"Why are there more people?" I asked Mars. "Who are they?"

"People you used to know," Mars said. "Hades asked them to help us defeat Hella and Nyx once and for all. Apparently, there hasn't been a war with these many gods since they killed you centuries ago."

After scrambling out of his lap, I stood to my feet and brushed the dirt off my pants. Then, I reached down, grabbed Mars's hands, and pulled him up. When he stood, he seized my hand and tugged me along out of the cave to meet the divine beings I couldn't quite remember.

But it didn't matter.

We were closer to Hella's kingdom, closer to finding Ares, closer to ending everything.

CHAPTER 29

Since last night, Marcel had come back every few hours to touch Hella until she came. She lay back on the bed, stripped naked, with Marcel between her legs.

First, he just ate her pussy until she was screaming in pleasure for him to stop.

Then, she had forced him to be inside her.

She faced me and spread her legs, forcing me to watch Marcel strip off his pants and crawl between her legs. He wouldn't look me in the face, could barely even look in my mere direction. His gaze was focused on the bed, his grip loose on the bedsheets beside her body.

Every time she came because of him, he lost a little bit of himself. I could tell by the way he hung his head lower, how his body became limper. His stoic personality had completely and utterly vanished.

Who the hell knew what she had done to him down here?

I hoped that one day, he would become angry enough to snap out of it.

I hoped that one day, he would kill Hella himself and break me out of here.

What broke my cold fucking heart the most—for him *and* for my sister—was that when he pulled out of her, his cum spilled from her pussy. She had gotten him to not only fuck her, but to come inside of her too.

Hella wanted him to do more than just break. Hella wanted to torture him. She must've known how much Charolette meant to Marcel if he was willing to die for her and spend eternity in the underworld to keep my sister alive.

Once Hella scurried off the bed, she crouched down next to my cage and reached in to touch me. "You'd better be taking it in, doggy, because you're next. The only woman you'll ever put your cum inside of again is me. And I will bear your children."

From the few hours that I had been here, I had learned to control myself. If I flipped and grasped the silver again, my wounds would reopen, and I would never get the fuck out of here to see Aurora again.

When Hella finally put on her clothes and left the room, Marcel did what he always did—put on his clothes and pulled the sheets off the bed to wash them. He walked around the room, lingering longer than usual, and placed some dirty clothes in the hamper.

"You don't mean it," I said, sitting in the middle of the cage so my skin didn't touch any silver. My wounds weren't healing here, and if I continued to try to get out, I would probably end up eventually killing myself. "I know that she's forcing you to do this."

Marcel didn't say anything.

"When I see Charolette, I'll explain everything to her," I said, taking back everything that I had told him the first time I saw him in Hella's room. "She won't hate you for what you've done. You've done it all for her."

Instead of walking out of the room without saying another word to me like he usually did, he lingered by the doorway as he held the hamper in his two hands. He should've left by now, but I knew that there was some of him still here, still aching for Charolette.

"If you keep sleeping with her," I started, swallowing hard, "you're going to fucking get her pregnant. You're going to have a kid with another woman and not with your own mate. You will despise that kid forever."

The hamper dropped from his hands, landing right on his bare toes, but he didn't even wince. His body seemed to not even react, nor belong to him anymore. Could he even feel down here? His body *was* ghostlike, after all.

"Don't you want to have a pup with Charolette, with your only mate?"

Marcel fell to his hands and knees in the middle of the room, his head hung low and his wavering gaze focused on the ground. "After what I've done, she'll never want to be with me again, no matter what you say to her."

It was the first few words he had spoken to me.

"That's not true," I said.

"I've been biting my tongue and doing this for her and for you," Marcel said. "You and Aurora deserve the fucking world. You guys have weakened Hella a great deal already, have led this war, and have had your baby ripped from your arms. Aurora's out there, waiting for you. She would be devastated to find out that Hella forced herself on you."

"Think about your-fucking-self, Marcel. I know you can be a selfish son of a bitch. So, be one for Charolette."

"You need to get out of here. Tonight," he said, ignoring me. "The guards change at four-thirty a.m. They're tired by four a.m.

You have half an hour to find a way out of the castle and past the guards of this kingdom."

"You're coming with me," I said.

"Don't worry about me," he said, sliding a key between the silver metal bars, his fingers skinnier and more fragile than Charolette's ever were, even when she was extremely sick. "I will never leave this place. Charolette's life is more important to me than my own."

"Oh, Marcel!" Hella called down the hallway.

Though I wanted to argue with him, I knew that I would never get anywhere. He wouldn't leave this place if I begged him to, not even if I tried to force him to leave the kingdom. Running outside this kingdom's territory and escaping would mean death to his mate.

Marcel stood to his feet, wiped all emotion off his face, and picked up the hamper. "If you ever see Charolette again, don't even mention my name. I don't want her to remember me because I have done nothing but betray her here."

CHAPTER 30

$\mathcal{A}$urora stayed by my side as we walked with our pack and the other gods toward Hella's kingdom. She laid a hand on her stomach almost instinctively and continued forward, glancing over at me every now and then.

She'd had a dream of our daughter last night, the same one that I must've had.

I stared down at my mate, knowing that I had missed so damn much of her pregnancy and that *we* were missing years of our daughter's life. Aurora had said that she looked to be much, much older. If our dreams were real time, then our daughter must be almost ten by now.

Almost a decade.

A fucking decade.

All because Hella was a bitch.

When—if—we returned, Aurora would be devastated. I hadn't even been able to see her reaction when Ares told her that we'd have a little girl, but I could tell that she wanted a pup so badly. I hoped that Ares had worshipped every inch of her body when she was pregnant and made her feel like the sexiest thing alive.

Because to an alpha, there was nothing sexier than our mates pregnant with our pups.

"I wish that I could've been there throughout your pregnancy with you," I said, brushing my hand over the pudge of fat where our baby once had been. The baby weight hadn't rolled off Aurora yet, and I wouldn't mind if it never did.

She was a fucking goddess either way.

"Being with only Ares during that time ..." Aurora smiled and let out a small chuckle. "Of course, he got all alpha male and protective over me, but you would've been so proud of him. He really tried hard to become sweeter and more caring to everyone around him."

"Really?" I asked, taken aback. "The hardheaded, easily angered Ares did that for you?"

She broke out into a grin. "Yes."

By the way she smiled and spoke about each of us, I could tell that we both still had pieces of her heart. She would never be whole unless we were all together again, until all of us returned to the Sanguine Wilds and watched our daughter grow up.

"We'll get out of here," I promised. "Soon."

"Soon. Then, maybe we'll get to see our girl," she said, becoming quiet for a few moments. "You know, we didn't even get to name her. We had a couple names picked out, but hadn't told anyone. We were waiting to see what she looked like to choose which name fit her best. When we do see her again, I fear that I'll know nothing about her."

Ruffles—who I'd *almost* forgotten had come down to the underworld—appeared at our feet and meowed. Her babies and her little husband were nowhere to be found, though. They seemed to come and go as they pleased, no matter how many times Aurora tried to keep her with us. Her fur was more ruffled than normal.

"*Meow*!" Ruffles purred, rubbing against me with a distinct scent that I could never forget.

"You smell like home," Aurora said, pulling Ruffles into her arms.

"*Meow*."

"No, Ruffles," Aurora said. "I'm still spending time with Mars. He's *my* mate."

"*Meow*!"

"No, he's not. You have Pringle."

"*Meow*!" Ruffles stuck her little snout up in the air, her eyes twinkling as they met mine. She batted Aurora's shoulder, scrambled in her arms, and then hopped through the air and over to me. She landed with a thud onto my chest. "*Meow*."

I gently rubbed under her chin until we approached Hella's property. The air became mustier and thicker. Fog sat heavily under the canopy of blackened trees, and brittle skeleton creatures patrolled about a mile ahead of us—too far to spot us, but far enough that I could smell them.

I had been here a couple times before, mainly to stake out the place with Helios and to come up with some sort of plan that always seemed to fall through. Nyx and Hella were too damn good together. We needed them separated.

After glancing over my shoulder to ensure that the gods still held Fenris in their possession, I looked back at Hella's castle and frowned. This wasn't going to be easy, especially because they had Ares as their prisoner. We could offer a fair trade—Ares for Fenris—but Ares would fucking kill me for that.

And we would have the disadvantage once more.

If only there was a way for him to destroy the castle from the inside out, we might be able to make this work. A captured Fenris was one that we needed to keep. If we released him, he might start trying to make Mom into a more powerful undead monster.

They would pin her against us.

They knew that I couldn't kill my own mother.

"What shall we do?" a goddess asked, crossing her arms.

"Wait until dusk?" someone suggested. "Then, rain hellfire down on them?"

"Yes," Hades said. "Right after the guards switch for the night."

"No," Aurora said. "We need help. We need more people. We will not be able to destroy their army without …" She paused, as if something had clicked in her head. "We won't be able to win without someone on the inside or Ares escaping and … and the harpies."

"How are we going to contact them all the way out here?" someone asked. "They only really reside around Hades's kingdom."

Aurora gulped. "I'll connect with the wolf I saved. I'll ask them to come."

"How are you going to do that?" Acesca asked her. "You need to conserve your power."

"I need to *ensure survival*," Aurora said, glancing up at me. "To see our baby again."

CHAPTER 31

AURORA

"No, absolutely not," Mars said, hurrying after me, back toward the camp we'd set up outside of Hella and Nyx's kingdom. "I'm not letting you drain yourself of energy. The last time this happened while I was with you, you almost fucking died."

"I'm aware," I said, thinking back to the cave when I had depleted all my energy and the hounds took Mars away from me. I had thought long and hard about how we would be able to survive down here, and this was the only option.

If I could summon not only the harpies, but also the wolves that had once been hounds that I saved only a few days ago, then we might have a chance. It might be easier to control the hounds working with Hella and Nyx and get them on our side.

There wasn't another way.

We were at Hella's doorstep. We were hours away from the greatest battle of our lives. We either stepped up now and gave it one last final push with all these gods on our side or we caved into the darkness and never saw our daughter again.

And I vowed to see her in real life one time.

Just one fucking time.

"Then, why do you insist on putting yourself in danger over and over again?!" Mars exclaimed, shaking his head and running a hand through his hair. "If you die down here, you will never be able to go back to the Sanguine Wilds."

"What?" I asked, face suddenly paling. "Not even if we kill Hella?"

Mars shook his head. "No."

"So, then ..." I paused, heart pounding. "You won't be able to come home?"

"I don't know," he whispered. "It works differently with me and Ares. Nothing like us has ever happened before, so I'm not sure what will happen. I might be able to return since I passed in the world above. Not here."

"Does everyone who dies here stay here, no matter what?"

Mars ran a hand through his hair. "I don't know, Aurora. All that matters is you conserving your energy. You need to be strong. I'm going to get you back to the Sanguine Wilds, no matter if I can go or not."

"No," I growled at my own mate. "What matters is, we end this war. Or else ... this all will be for nothing. All the deaths down here, all the people we left in the world above, Marcel sacrificing his life for Charolette ..."

"What do you mean?" Mars interrupted. "Marcel is here?"

"Marcel ..." I started, eyes widening slightly.

Mars didn't know about how sick his sister had become after he died. He didn't know that she had been days away from death right before we left, but Marcel must've successfully switched lives with her.

"What happened to him?"

"He's down in the underworld," I said, taking his hands in

mine. "Charolette became extremely sick. Her chemo wasn't working. The doctors gave up on her, and she gave up on herself. She was about to start hospice right before we left, but we found out that Marcel could …" I swallowed hard, feeling so much shame and guilt for keeping it a secret from Charolette. "We found out that Marcel could exchange his life to keep her alive."

Mars's lips parted, disbelief washing over his face. "He sacrificed his life for her."

"For his mate," I whispered. "Like you did for me. I refuse to let you both have died for nothing. We need to kill Hella for good this time, so things can go back to normal. We need to get us all out of here. We deserve to be happy for once."

After a few long moments of staring at me, Mars nodded. "Okay."

"Okay?" I asked, brows furrowed.

"Okay," he confirmed.

Once I knew he was on board, I walked over to Acesca and knelt by her side to start summoning the harpies and the wolves that I'd saved. "Don't listen to Mars or any of the other gods. Only stop me when you know my body can take no more. I trust you and your health abilities."

When she nodded, I sat back against a tree and closed my eyes, ready to summon as many friendly hounds and harpies as I could. I didn't know how I would do it, but I vowed to figure out a way. Tonight would be the end of this war. For good.

ARES

Moments.

It was mere moments before I had to leave.

I sat in the cage in Hella's bedroom and turned the key over and over in my palm. While I wanted to get out of here so badly, I didn't know how the fuck I could just leave Marcel here to rot for the rest of eternity. It wasn't fair.

But none of this was fucking fair. It wasn't fair that Mars hadn't been able to witness Aurora's pregnancy. It wasn't fair that Aurora hadn't even gotten to see our daughter's face before Medusa turned us to stone. It wasn't fair that we were missing our daughter's life.

There was no way that I could sit in this cage for another night. I needed to get out of here sometime tonight, and Marcel had risked his damn *life* to get me this key. The least that I could do was use it, right?

When the clock dinged, signaling that I had fifteen minutes until the guards changed, I pushed the key into the lock on the dog cage and twisted it. The bars creaked as I opened the door, but the silver suddenly wasn't burning my skin.

I quickly crawled out of the cage and stood to my feet, stretching for the first time in what seemed like days now. My entire body ached, my muscles sore from sitting in the same position. My wolf howled inside my head at the freedom he'd been granted.

Find mate, he said in my head. *Escape and find mate now.*

After finding some clothes that wouldn't draw attention to me, I stuffed the key into my pocket and walked to the door. When I grasped the handle, a pain shot through my chest. I shouldn't leave Marcel here.

It might've been something that I would've done in the past, but not anymore.

Once these monsters had killed Mars, I had to fill in for him. I had to be that same man for Aurora. I had to be strong and loving, even when I didn't love my-fucking-self. I had to fucking care more about her and more about my pack because I was the alpha.

Alphas didn't leave their comrades behind.

Ever.

Aurora, my wolf howled. *Find Aurora.*

I swallowed hard, knowing that this wasn't the right thing to do, and opened the door. After checking to ensure that the coast was clear, I stepped out of the room and hurried down the same hallway that Hella's guards had brought me down.

Sitting in that cage for hours—days maybe—I'd had to replay something in my head to believe that, one day, I would get out alive. So, I had replayed the escape route that I would take once I found a way out. I remembered everything after Nyx had pulled me out of that dream state.

Sneaking down the hallways, I peered in every room in hopes to find Marcel. I didn't want to leave alone. I wanted to take him away with me, though part of me knew that I would never be able to, or else Hella would kill Charolette in the worst way possible.

Once I made it down a back staircase, I glanced around the corner and spotted my exit—a large door, guarded by two tired-looking, demonic hellhounds. Outside the windows, all I could see was the thick fog, similar to how Hound Territory looked.

I didn't know how big Hella's army really was, but the fog was thicker than I had ever seen it. By the looks of it, her army was two, or maybe three, times the size of ours. Hell, she could raise people from the fucking dead.

If she killed all the people in my pack, she could instantly use them against us. One of these days, she would use *Mom* against me, and I didn't know if I would be able to handle that. How would I be able to kill Mom? How could I do that to my own family member?

One of the hellhounds closed his tired eyes, his snout falling as if he was dozing off. Knowing that I only had one fucking chance, I took a deep breath and stepped out of the shadows to sneak over to him.

Halfway to the door, I heard footsteps. I hid behind a large bookcase and glanced over as Marcel followed Hella into the grand room. She had him on a leash—on a fucking leash—and dragged him along after her, forcing him to wear nothing but a look of shame.

My chest tightened, my canines lengthening. I wanted to kill her so badly.

Find Aurora, my wolf ordered again.

This time, I ignored him. This time, *I had* to ignore him.

Marcel grabbed the chains and stopped in the middle of the hallway. "Please, let up. The chains are burning my skin."

Hella looked over at him in pure disgust and tugged on the chains harder to pull him closer, and then she smacked him hard across the cheek. He went flying to the floor, his muscles depleted of any energy. He looked tortured.

"I don't give a fuck how you feel," she growled. "Get up. You're pathetic."

From the chains, there were deep burn marks on his skin, so deep that I could see the reddened muscle and blood pouring down his forearms. He whimpered and stood. Every step that he took to follow her looked like it hurt worse and worse.

His wolf howled, desperate for someone to save him, desperate to see his mate again.

When they disappeared into another hallway, I stepped out from the darkness and glanced toward the sleeping hellhound at the doorway. I needed to get out of here. I needed to find Aurora.

I need to stop this.

Find mate now! my wolf called.

But I couldn't listen to him anymore. I turned right around, and from the first step I took, I had a bad feeling that this wasn't the right decision, but still, I headed back up the staircase and down the hallways toward Hella's room.

Because an alpha didn't leave anyone behind.

Marcel had been through everything with me since we were children. He had loved my sister so much that he decided to die for her. He had sacrificed everything for me so I could spend my life with my mate.

Leaving him didn't sit well for me, for the god of war.

Tonight, we would end this.

CHAPTER 33

MARS

*A*urora sat on the grass, surrounded by the other gods and goddesses as well as her friend, Acesca. With her eyes closed, Aurora furrowed her brows and clenched her small hands into tight fists as she still tried to connect with the wolves and harpies.

I stared at my mate, hoping to the gods that she wasn't willingly putting herself in danger by doing this. I didn't know the first thing about how she was able to connect with the hounds and the wolves, but it was something special.

Something I hoped wouldn't come bite her in the ass.

"I'm so close," she mumbled, jaw twitching.

A few silent moments passed, not even the chattiest of gods making a sound. I swallowed and tried to calm my racing heart. I wanted this to be over already. I wanted her to be safe by my side.

Suddenly, her face paled, and her head snapped back, so she stared right up to the sky, except her eyes were still closed. When her body seized briefly, I sat up taller and rubbed my hands together, looking over at Acesca, who didn't seem worried.

"Is she okay?" I asked, nervous as hell.

I had just gotten her back. I couldn't lose her again.

Acesca felt her pulse and nodded. "Just a bit of an increase in heart rate. She can expend more energy before she passes out. I'll make sure to pull her out before then, but"—she gnawed on the inside of her cheek—"don't disrupt her while she's in here."

It was easier said than done.

Pain shot through my chest as she shook slightly. The veins in her neck became more pronounced, crawling up the column of her throat toward her eyes. Her eyes moved around underneath her eyelids, as if searching for something.

Incoherent words tumbled out of her mouth, almost sounding like an ancient language or something similar to the words in Medusa's journal. I didn't even think that she'd understood it when we were there, reading the journal.

Maybe she had.

"So close," Aurora finally said.

Almost at the same time, her body fell back against the dirt, and her head smacked against the ground. I hurried over to her and cradled her head, gently rubbing it and trying to find any bumps.

She seized harder and faster, her limbs moving uncontrollably. I called out her name. I tried to get her to come back to me. I tried to connect with her through the mind link, but nothing. Absolutely nothing.

"Acesca," I growled. "Do something."

Acesca crawled over to us and placed her fingers on Aurora's neck, brows drawn together. "She can go for a longer period. She told me not to pull her out until I knew that her body couldn't control itself anymore."

"She can't!" I growled. "Look at her."

"She can go longer," Acesca said, voice soft and head bowed.

"I'm sorry, Alpha Mars, but she can go for longer. She can connect with them. She said it herself that she's close to connection. Please, let her."

But how could I just let her? This was my mate, for crying out loud.

If Ares came back and found her dead ...

If she died in my arms ...

I wouldn't be able to live with myself.

Distantly, the sound of howls erupted through the air. All the gods glanced over their shoulders and deep into the woods toward the direction of footsteps and flapping wings, and then we all saw the pack that Aurora had saved the other day, plus others.

Suddenly, Aurora's body stopped convulsing. She opened her eyes and stared into the woods behind me, her irises glowing the soft colors of the dawn and her lips curled into a small smile. "They're here, and they're willing to help."

With them, we would double our army. With them, we would have a fighting chance.

AURORA

Hundreds of harpies and wolves—hellhounds and undead—poured out of the forest. They surrounded us from all angles, from around us and above us, coming in by the freaking droves to fight with a bunch of people from the Sanguine Wilds and gods.

Tears welled up in my eyes as I relaxed in Mars's arms. It had been so difficult to connect to them through the mind link, but I had done it. Not only that, but I'd also inspired them to come fight for *our* cause.

Hella had hurt one too many people and monsters here. We would end that tonight.

As the final few harpies trickled in, I shifted in Mars's arms to get a good look at everyone. There were people here that even I didn't recognize, wolves I hadn't healed, nor had I saved. People who recognized me as Dawn, not Aurora.

When everyone finally surrounded us, I stared around and shuffled to my feet. Mars stood next to me and held my hand to steady my slightly trembling body. I still felt a bit too drained of energy for the second time in the past few days, but this had to be done.

"We are ending this tonight," I said to the creatures and gods from the underworld.

A fury of whispers erupted through the forest, accompanied by head nods.

"One thing that must be done," I started, taking a deep breath to calm myself, "is to get Nyx and Hella away from each other. Their powers are far too strong to use together. Hella has some brute strength left in her, and Nyx will make us all go crazy. We lost Ares that way."

Murmurs broke out among the species again, but Mars growled to silence them.

"Yes, it's true," I confirmed, hoping that what I was about to say was accurate. "Ares was captured, but don't let that get you down. He will do what he needs to do inside Hella's home to escape and aid us in any way that he can."

After taking another step forward, I smiled tensely at them all. I hoped that tonight wouldn't be another night that I lost Mars, though. I couldn't lose both of them or else I would be broken to pieces. We needed to get home so badly. Our girl was growing incredibly fast.

"We already have Fenris locked and chained up," I announced. "He is our prisoner, and we will use him wisely. We will either end his life or we will use him to advance us in this war—to *win* this war. No matter what, we *will win*."

"Taking Nyx away," Mars stepped in, "will be a collaborative effort. But we especially need the harpies to bring Nyx elsewhere. Is that possible?"

The woman I'd helped before flew forward a few feet and nodded. "Yes."

"What do we do next?" another god chimed.

"Once we get them apart, I will try to free those hounds and hellhounds from Hella's hold," I said. "I know that we will have to kill some of them, even your old comrades and friends whose minds have been taken over. But sacrifices must be made."

Sacrifice was all I seemed to know lately.

"I know that we've all tried to fight this war before, and we lost." I glanced around, heart racing. "Do not fear them. They will thrive off of it. They know that they have the upper hand. They know they have captured a god. They know that they are stronger together. But we know our strength. We know that we refuse to be part of this torture anymore."

All I could think about was finding Ares again and getting the hell out of here. I wouldn't let Hella stop me or anyone else from having a good life.

"Tonight, we run. Tonight, we live!" I said, staring out into the forest that surrounded Hella's kingdom and watching as the sea of gods, goddesses, hounds, and monsters nodded in agreement.

They all looked ready to fight, to survive.

I shifted into my wolf, feeling the power swell inside me, and ran through the woods to lead our pack of warriors. Mars sprinted beside me, his body close to mine and his eyes glowing the most intense shade of gold.

Tonight, we would find our other half.

Tonight, we would have the war of all wars.

Tonight, we would kill Hella, like she had done to me.

CHAPTER 35

ARES

It hurt me to walk back into Hella's room, open the cage, and willingly get back inside it. I wanted to see Aurora so badly, but I couldn't let Marcel dwindle away like this. If we wanted to win this war, we needed someone from the inside. We needed Marcel and his strength.

Since I had been out of the cage, my scars and the wounds on my body had healed significantly. Not entirely, but enough for me to feel like I actually had some of my innate strength back.

As I listened to Hella's footsteps down the hall, I cursed at myself and placed the chain around my neck again. I didn't lock it on purpose, wanting to be able to get out of it as soon as I needed to. I refused to let Marcel go down like this.

Hella walked into the room, dragging Marcel in with her. The burns on his body had gotten worse within the past twenty minutes, the skin completely peeled off and the muscle a blazing red underneath the chains.

"Good," she said, glancing over at me. "You're awake."

Marcel snapped his head toward me and widened his eyes, as if to ask why the fuck I hadn't left yet. He had risked his life to get me that key and to give me any sort of information about how to get out of here.

Now, I would risk mine to save him.

After shoving Marcel up onto the bed, Hella crouched by the front of the cage and stuck her finger between the bars to brush them against my cheek. "I know I promised that you'd get to have me next, but Marcel has been so bad tonight. I need to punish him. But you can have me after. Don't worry."

I wasn't fucking worried about having her or not.

I wanted her dead.

She turned away from the cage and peeled off her blouse, leaving her top half bare. Marcel tore his gaze away from me and looked down at his lap, tears welling up in his eyes. All the times before this, he had been so strong. Tonight, he looked so broken.

Charolette would hate to see him like this.

"Stay strong," I said through the mind link. *"I'm going to get you out of here."*

Marcel didn't respond to me; I didn't even know if he could hear me. Either way, I sat in my cage and let my rage build higher and higher. As far as I knew, the only person who could kill another god was Nyx, but I would try tonight.

I would do everything in my power to end Hella's life. And if I couldn't, then I would take her as prisoner, wrap these silver chains around *her* body so she couldn't do magic, break Marcel out of here, and find Aurora.

"Do you want to tell Ares what you did today?" Hella asked Marcel, shimmying out of her pants and crawling up onto the bed with him. She straddled his waist and placed her hands on his dwindling abdomen. "Hmm?"

"No," Marcel said.

One single word that fucking engaged Hella.

She wrapped his hands around his fragile throat and grasped

it hard. "You know what will happen if you disrespect me again. I didn't have to accept your wishes. I could've let that *mate* of yours die in the Sanguine Wilds. And I still can."

Marcel squirmed underneath her, that golden fire back in his eyes.

"One more slipup, and I'll kill Charolette."

That was the last straw. I yanked off my chain from around my neck, took it in my hands, threw open the dog cage door, and jumped onto the bed with them. After wrapping the chain around Hella's neck, I squeezed as hard as I could, my muscles feeling like they would burst out of my skin.

Hella continued to struggle underneath me and continued to choke Marcel harder, but I refused to let her have him. He wouldn't die tonight, and Charolette wouldn't either. I closed my eyes and thought about everything that had led to this moment.

About Mars dying.

About us leaving our baby.

About Hella capturing me.

Her hands slipped from around Marcel's neck, coming up to the chains to pull on them. But it seemed like these magic chains *also* stopped her from using her strength. She'd said that she had made chains strong enough to hold me back, but she'd failed to mention that these chains also affected her too.

"Ares!" she shouted. "Stop it!"

But I refused to stop. I tugged harder on them, so hard that she fell limp on the bed on top of Marcel and stopped struggling completely. I cocooned her in the chains and shoved her into the dog cage, and then I looked over at Marcel.

"Get your clothes on," I said. "We're getting out of here."

"But she'll kill Charolette."

"She can't use her powers in these chains," I said. "I couldn't. Charolette will be safe for now. She has more life in the Sanguine Wilds to enjoy because of you. Now, hurry, Marcel. We don't have much time."

CHAPTER 36

MARS

One moment, we were gathered just outside of Hella and Nyx's kingdom, planning on how we would separate Nyx from Hella, how we would get onto their property with the hundreds of hounds guarding it, and how the fuck we'd get Ares back.

The next moment, hounds and evil gods were running toward us at full speed. They were coming from all angles, all directions, everywhere.

I grabbed Aurora's hand and watched them, my heart pounding inside my chest.

It was now or never.

We would kill them now, or we would never kill them. We wouldn't get another chance.

A hound jumped through the air and latched his teeth into Hades, who sent his three-headed dog to rip it to shreds. As if they were ready for this, the other gods and goddesses sprang into action to fight off as many hounds as they could handle.

They either knew we were coming, had spotted us … or something had happened inside the castle with Ares and Marcel and they had become extra careful about monitoring the forest just outside their lands.

We had been cautious up until now, which meant …

Ares must have done something.

"Go!" Hades shouted. "We'll hold off as many as we can. Take the harpies and find Nyx."

Without having to be told twice, I grabbed Aurora's hand and tugged her through a crowd of enemies fighting until their death. They were all mindless, under the control of Hella and Nyx, using their bodies as shields and weapons.

Hundreds of them pushed by us as we came to a clearing right before the castle.

"I can't go any further, Mars," Aurora said, grabbing my hand tighter. "If we're going to win, then we need some of these hounds by our side. I hate seeing them so blinded and not in control, being used by these gods. I need to help them."

"I'm not leaving you alone," I said, my chest tightening. "You're my mate. I need to protect you."

She gently grasped my face. "Then, protect me by finding Nyx and having the harpies fly her the fuck out of here. We need to get her as far away from here as possible. Without you, they won't know what to do with her."

"Don't you want to kill her?" I asked, tucking some hair behind her ear. "For what she's done to you in your past life? She killed you with her bare hands. You deserve to rip her to pieces."

Aurora glanced at the hounds fighting around us. "I need to help them."

"Aurora," I whispered, my heart fucking shattering.

After standing on her toes, she pressed her lips on mine and kissed me hard. "I fucking love you. I will always love you. Please, go protect us and our family. We can't let the hounds kill us or else … our daughter dies. Don't do that to me."

Just hearing the heartbreak in her voice, I leaned down to kiss her one last time and then leaned my forehead against hers. I didn't want to do this. I didn't want to leave her. But … I needed to do this for us. I needed to trust that she was strong enough.

When she dropped her hands from me, my entire body felt cold. I swallowed hard and stepped backward and toward the harpies. "I fucking love you, Aurora. And I will not lose you again. I will find you when this is all over, and we will go see our daughter."

"We will," Aurora said softly.

Once she disappeared through the crowd of enemies, I let out a deep breath, my muscles tense, and glanced toward the sky, where the flock of harpies flew around. Some had gathered above me, one swooping down and standing in front of me.

"We think that we've spotted Nyx's wing of the castle," she said, lifting her wing and pointing toward the north. "Do you see those birds, right across the way?"

Three birds who flew relatively close to the castle suddenly stopped flapping their wings and fell from the sky. My body froze, and I found myself swallowing hard again. If what I remembered from Aurora was true, then Nyx was in there, using her power against these harpies.

"We have to go," I said.

The bird lifted herself into the air and flew inches above me, sinking her claws into my shoulders and pulling me into the air. "Hold on tightly. I'll bring you as close as I can without getting into her range of magic."

We flew there through the air, the wind whipping my hair back, and we scanned the forest from a bird's-eye view to see if I could spot where Nyx was hiding in the building. A shadow moved from the farthest window toward the next one, heading through the building east to west.

"There!" I shouted.

"Catch her!" a harpy cawed to the group.

Five harpies flew into the building, smashing the concrete to pieces and demolishing the siding. Giant pieces of concrete fell from the castle, destroying the floor underneath it and making Nyx fall to the ground.

Almost immediately, she pushed herself up to her feet and continued to hurry toward where Hella must've been inside the building. She turned around, running backward, and lifted one hand to the sky, taking control of the birds and making them fall with a hard thud.

"Don't let her see you," I said to the harpy carrying me.

Nyx ran toward a building on the west that had some of the lights on, and in my gut, I felt that Hella was definitely in there with Ares and Marcel. I didn't know what the fuck they had done, if they had done anything, but I wanted—needed—to protect my pack as much as I could.

"Get as close to her as you can. We need to stop her before she gets into that building."

The bird swooped down and flew near to the ground while Nyx scanned the air and tried to control more of the harpies. But not us.

Today, we would destroy her and everything that she stood for.

CHAPTER 37

AURORA

ollapsing to my knees, I stared up into the sky as harpies collided with the concrete palace at the east wing. Mars drifted through the sky, in the claws of another powerful female harpy, directing her toward Nyx's figure.

I wanted to run after them. I wanted to kill her.

But I had a bigger part in all this.

Hounds tore their teeth into wolves. Blood splattered everywhere. I latched on to one, holding him as hard as I could from behind so he couldn't struggle that intensely, and silently whispered some foreign words off my tongue.

Like I had done with the other unfriendly hounds, I tried to get him on my side. I tried to pull him out of Nyx's strong hold, but I couldn't. I fucking couldn't. With her being distracted, she should've had her attention elsewhere. Her energy had to have a limit, right?

The hound escaped my arms and turned on me, baring its bloody fangs and growling lowly. I focused on him and only him, grabbing at his face once more. He clawed me across the chest, across the stomach, the thigh and calf.

Yet I persisted.

I needed to get through to him. I needed something. Just from one of the hounds. If I could take control of one of them, then we might be able to do this thing. It was just getting harder and harder. I didn't have as much energy as I had the first time. I had just depleted my energy completely, summoning the harpies and the freed wolves.

"Don't push yourself, Kitten," Ares—yes, Ares—said through the mind link. *"I'm coming."*

My wolf purred. Warmth spread throughout my chest. I didn't know where he was or if he could see me—maybe I was just imagining it all—but he had given me what I needed to push through the pain of this hound's claws cutting through my flesh.

After scanning the forest and not finding anyone, I turned back to the wolf and closed my eyes. All I could feel was the blood pouring out of my wounds and even more claws sinking into my flesh from all angles. At this rate and with exhaustion nearing, I didn't know if my wounds would heal anytime soon.

It could be years.

Still, I knew deep down that my mates would still love me.

So, I continued and held the hound tighter. "Please," I whispered, surprisingly staying calm. "Please, see the light, see the dawn. I need you to get out of Nyx's hold. You are not who she tells you that you are. You're good."

Nothing.

"Aurora!" someone shouted out loud.

But I couldn't tear myself away from the hound. I needed to get to him, needed to make sure that he knew that he had been different from this in a past life, that this person and wolf that he was today wasn't the real him.

When I reopened my eyes, all I saw was blood pouring out of

the wounds in my body. I forced myself to stare into the hound's eyes and look deep into him.

"You are so powerful," I whispered.

Another slash across my face.

"You are so much stronger than she is."

Another slash across my abdomen, where my baby had once been.

"You can escape from her."

Another slash across my neck.

Then … he stopped moving completely. His eyes faded to a lighter color, a less hazy color. I beamed at him, not caring that he had almost killed me. This was progress. Slow progress, but progress.

"You're doing great," I whispered, grabbing his snout. "Take control back."

He shook his head, as if he didn't want to hear what I was saying, but when I brushed my thumb across his snout, he howled. And not in the way that hounds did when they were about to kill someone.

In the way that … he realized who he really was.

CHAPTER 38

ARES

"Where's the prison?" I asked Marcel, once he was clothed. I pulled Hella out of the cage and threw her over my shoulder to carry her more easily. That bitch seemed to like it, too, because while she still squirmed in my arms and was bound up, she tried to touch every part of my body.

Marcel nodded down a hallway toward a set of stairs. "This way."

After hurrying down, Marcel grabbed my shoulder when we settled on the landing and pulled me behind a door to hide us. He pressed a hand over my mouth and Hella's, so we both couldn't speak.

A couple moments later, about ten hellhounds ran down the stairs and out one of the side doors that led to the land behind the castle. I tried to get a glimpse of the outside and found nothing but chaos happening.

Wolves and gods and hellhounds. Blood splattering. Bones breaking. People howling.

"Stay strong, Aurora," I whispered through the mind link.

I didn't know where Aurora was, but my wolf could tell that she was close. Through the mind link, I heard her thoughts racing about a million miles per second. She was worried about something—maybe about me. I needed to get out of here and find her.

But right now, she was the only thing getting me through this hell down here. She didn't know how much I needed her, nor how strong she was. And I hoped that Mars saw her strength too. I hoped he didn't think she wasn't strong enough to defeat Nyx on her own.

Once the guards passed, Marcel let go of our mouths and hiked a thumb back toward the door. "Did you see that?" he asked, eyes widening. "They're here. We have to go help them. They won't be able to defeat all those hounds alone."

Swallowing hard, I stared at the door. Aurora and Mars had to be right outside, in the midst of the fight too. But if one thing was certain about all this, it was that we couldn't go out and fight them, no matter how much we wanted to.

We needed to get Hella as far away from them as possible. Maybe then she wouldn't be able to control the hounds as strongly. Maybe then the hounds would finally be weaker, and we would finally be able to win this raging war.

I wasn't sure if it would happen, but we had to try.

As Marcel went toward the door, I grabbed his shoulder. Guilt washed over me because I doubted that Marcel had seen the outdoors in a long time. Hella had had him cooped up and chained to this house since he had been down here.

I wanted him to taste freedom again, but at the same time, I wanted him to be able to see Charolette again. I wanted him to see his mate. I wanted him to get back to the Sanguine Wilds and be happy.

Because no matter how much he'd tried to convince me, he wasn't staying down here.

No fucking way would I do that to him or to Charolette.

"We have to lock Hella up in the prison," I said, clenching my jaw as howls echoed through the room. "It's the only way to help them. Let them take care of Nyx, and we will take care of this bitch."

Confusion and hurt crossed Marcel's face. He hadn't been able to fight since he'd left the Sanguine Wilds with us, and he had been born and bred to be a warrior, to fight in battle after battle, to kill.

"Think about Charolette," I said.

Marcel finally nodded and pointed down another staircase. "We have about four more floors to go. If we keep heading down here, it's the fastest route, but there will be more hellhounds and warriors that we'll need to keep an eye out for."

After nodding, I followed him down the flights of stairs. Every floor, we had to hide behind another door as more and more hellhounds and hounds piled out of the castle to join the fight outside. We needed to block more of Hella's power before she summoned *every* hound to fight.

If she did, we would lose this war, and I would lose my mate. No doubt about that.

Once six more hounds passed, we finally made it to the prison door. Marcel easily knocked out the two hellhounds that guarded the door and grabbed the key to the prison from his back pocket. He thrust it into the door.

As soon as the door opened, I could feel the intense searing and pain from the barrels of silver in the room. I didn't know how much was in here, but it was enough to make my knees tremble. Maybe this was her plan all along.

"Dump her over here," Marcel said, opening a cage in the back of the prison.

Every inch of the cage was laced with some kind of metal that seemed to repel gods, even me. It was worse than silver. The mere air in this room felt like knives cutting and sliding into my skin.

Once I dumped her onto the ground, I took the chains that I had already placed around her body and replaced them with these stronger ones that would bind her here forever. As soon as I stepped back, thoughts of another life rushed through my mind.

This was where they'd trapped Aurora.

This was where they'd tortured Aurora.

This was where they'd killed Aurora.

My hands balled into tight fists, and I gritted my teeth.

Before I could rip her to pieces, Marcel grabbed my shoulder and pulled me out of the room. "You will never be able to kill her. She's far too strong, especially with all those wolves. They feed off her the same way that she feeds off their energy."

I stepped back and glared at her in the cell, looking so broken and beaten.

Good.

"So, we wait," I said, hating the thought, but knowing that it was the only way.

"We wait."

CHAPTER 39

MARS

The harpies surrounded Nyx from all directions, swooping down around her, scratching at her body and cutting her, making it so she couldn't move. I pulled myself up from the claws of the harpy who held me, swung around, and sat on her back so it'd be easier for her.

"Tell them to grab her and fly her far away," I said, leaning down to speak in her ear.

"Will do," she said to me before cawing at the others in another language.

After a couple moments, the others cawed back, and four harpies flew down to grab Nyx by the limbs. They seized her body and took flight in a tight flock of birds, drifting over the horizon and heading toward somewhere—hopefully far, far away from here.

"They're heading to our home in the forest," she said, following her flock from behind in a slower direction, taking one last swoop around the battlefield. "It's far enough away from here that, hopefully, she won't be able to use her powers."

She continued talking, but my eyes landed on Aurora, who was lying in the middle of the battlefield. Her arms and legs and chest and body were covered with open wounds. She was bleeding profusely. And she looked drained of energy as more wolves ran at her.

I grasped some feathers in my fists and clenched my jaw. *"Kitten, stay strong."*

For a moment, she looked around, tired. The next moment, she glanced up at me through teary eyes and smiled.

"Take her away," Aurora said. *"Don't worry about me. I can handle it down here."*

And while I so desperately wanted to save her, I needed to remember that Aurora wasn't the helpless woman I'd found in the forest long ago. Hell, she was never helpless. But now, she was stronger and faster and more loving than I could ever be.

"She'll be safe," the harpy said to me, flying us away and toward her home. "Believe."

Believe.

Reluctantly, I tore my gaze away from my mate and focused on the sight ahead of us. I couldn't think about Aurora, nor could I worry about her. We needed to get this done and over with now, and we were so fucking close.

"Fly faster," I said.

The harpy flew faster to catch up with her flock, but they seemed like they were nowhere to be found. I stared down through the trees, hoping to spot them to see if they had landed earlier than expected.

"There!" I shouted, pointing to a clearing. "Right there."

After a couple moments, the harpy carrying me suddenly fell right out of the air. Her wings stopped flapping, her heavy body descending at an alarming pace—a pace that signified that she didn't have control of her body anymore.

I braced for impact and scanned the forest, catching Nyx standing in front of all the other harpies, who seemed to be dropping out of thin air too. Once we collided with the dirt, my body rolled four times, and I came to a stop.

Everything in me ached like fucking hell, but I refused to let her control me too. She tried to get in like she had last time. She tried to show me images of my daughter and what I'd left back home. But I refused to accept them.

They were lies fabricated from her ugly head.

Despite her strength, I stood up and bared my teeth at her. "I'm going to kill you."

"You're strong, Mars," she said, smirking. "Almost as strong as your mate."

"Maybe you're just not strong enough," I said, stepping forward and lengthening my nails into sharp talons. "Maybe you've exceeded your strength this time, Nyx. You're too far away from those hellhounds to control them any longer, and now, you can't control me."

She cackled menacingly. "Never underestimate the power of a goddess, especially one of the underworld. We always have a backup plan, a plan B in case someone—like you—tries to fuck up our day."

"You have no backup plan," I said between gritted teeth. "Hella won't help you. Fenris won't help you. Your wolves won't help you. You're all alone this time. It's just god against god, and I will kill you."

"I'm never alone," she said, glancing over my shoulder and smirking even wider. "I've always got someone willing to follow me through the depths of hell, just to kill her own son."

My entire body froze, a distinct scent drifting through my nostrils. "What did you say?" I asked, my voice barely coming out because I knew that scent. I had grown up with that scent. That scent belonged to my mother.

I turned around and stood face-to-face with a skin-and-bones monster I'd once called Mom.

CHAPTER 40

MARS

I stared at Mom in horror.

Nothing but bones. Nothing but eyes as dark and as deadly as Nyx's. Nothing but hatred and anger toward me. They had raised her from the dead and made her into a monster—a fucking monster. How could they have done such a thing?

Before I could react, Mom lunged at me and swiped sharp claws across my face diagonally. I stood silent and unmoving, not wanting to lay a hand on my mother. I had cried and begged for years for her to come back.

Now, I would have to kill her. It was the only way.

"Mom," I whispered as she continued to cut through my flesh. "Mom, it's me."

Yet she didn't care as she slashed and cut and bruised and broke her own son. She didn't even recognize me, and I didn't blame her for it. It had been over a damn decade since I'd last seen her. And she didn't have any mind or memories anymore.

"Please, Mom," I whispered, desperately thinking of my family back home.

I had to sever all ties, all bonds with my own mother.

What would Dad think when I went back to the Sanguine Wilds and told him? What about Charolette? Would they hate me for meeting Mom again and killing her with my two bare hands? Would I always be to blame?

Every time I closed my eyes to think, all I could hear was Mom's weak voice drifting through my ears as Fenris raped her and I stood in the closet, staring with wide eyes and not aiding her years ago.

Why didn't I fucking help her?

Mom jumped at me again, this time her claws coming dangerously close to ripping out my throat. By the second, she was becoming more violent. By the second, she was getting closer and closer to ending me for good.

I needed to stop this now.

Just as Mom leaped in my direction, I stuck my hand out and grabbed her throat. "Mom."

She wildly thrashed around in my hold, shoving and throwing her body back and forth, growling in agony. There was no sign of her own soul left inside her body. It was all corruption and pain and Nyx.

"I'm sorry," I whispered, just about to crush her to death.

But then she said, "Me too."

Before I snapped her neck, I stopped and stared, wide-eyed, at her. "What?" I whispered.

Suddenly, she stopped moving and fell limp in my arms. "I'm sorry for everything."

Her voice was stronger this time, but ... somehow, it didn't sound like hers. Or at least, it didn't sound like I remembered it. It had been years ago though since I'd last heard her speak. Maybe she really had sounded so broken.

Or maybe ...

Maybe this wasn't her at all.

With Mom still in my hold, I turned around just in time to see Nyx rushing at me from behind, about to stab me in the back and kill me right here and now. I dropped Mom and jumped back, facing off against two strong enemies.

It wasn't how I'd expected today to go. I glanced around at the harpies who were still in a trance and ground my teeth together. Whatever happened here today, I needed to kill both Mom and Nyx.

I needed to do it for my family, for the people who loved me, for my daughter.

Just as they both sprung at me once more, an echo of howls rumbled through the woods. I froze and let the two enemies jump on me, fear rushing through my body.

Nyx had brought the hounds here. Nyx had somehow summoned them all to come for me.

Tonight, I would die.

CHAPTER 41

"*R*un!" I shouted through the forest and to the hounds. "Kill her!"

I hurried to keep up, my legs trembling and weak, but my mind strong. It took everything inside me to make all those hounds believe in me and believe that there was a better life out there for them. But I had done it.

They were no longer bound by Hella or by Nyx. Now, they were free.

"Kill her!" I shouted with tears in my eyes, slowing down slightly. "Kill Nyx!"

It seemed to be the only thing that I could say. I didn't have it inside me to think about anything other than turning Nyx's wolves against her and letting them shred her to pieces. I didn't know if they'd be able to do it alone, but I wanted them to try.

They had been captured and enslaved to her for centuries. They deserved to finally taste freedom. They deserved to finally see what it felt like to kill their maker. They deserved to get back at her after all these long and tortuous years.

From afar, I spotted Mars being attacked by a wolf and Nyx. And while my legs wanted to give out, I pushed further and faster, tears streaming down my cheeks from the pain shooting through my body.

I needed him. I needed him more than anything.

She wouldn't take him away from me.

"Mars!" I shouted.

Mars glanced over his shoulder at me and mouthed, *You came for me.*

"Of course I came for you," I whispered through the mind link. *"I'll always come for you."*

With a sudden urgency in his eyes, Mars ripped Nyx off him and hurled her halfway across the forest. She landed against a tree, the tree cracking and breaking on impact. Then, she stood up and dusted herself off, finally glancing around her.

For the first time, I saw fear in her eyes. She held her hands up to try to stop the wolves from attacking her, to try to control them. But I had already freed their minds, and I refused to let them be slaves again.

They might've not been human by any means or true wolves. But they were beings who cared and loved and wanted more for themselves and their families than to be bound to the underworld forever.

"Forward!" I shouted to them. "Kill her."

As they continued, my legs gave out underneath me. I tumbled to the ground and desperately tried to stand back up, but I had completely depleted my energy. I struggled on my hands and knees, watching as Mars faced a monster that was nothing but bones.

While I wanted to give her mind back too, I knew that I didn't have the energy. I knew that I wouldn't be able to make her believe in something that she couldn't anymore. Most skin-and-bone monsters' and hounds' minds had faded centuries ago down here, their bodies quickly following.

"I don't think I can help her, Mars," I whispered through the mind link. *"I'm sorry. I don't think I can. My energy is exhausted, and I—"*

"I know, Kitten," he whispered back to me, taking the woman in his hand by the throat and staring at her through teary eyes himself. *"I would do anything for you, Aurora—anything. Don't lift another finger."*

And with that, he snapped her neck and ended her life. Then, he fell to his knees and picked up her bones in his hands, mouthing the word, *Mom,* over and over again.

More hounds flooded into the forest, blocking my view of him. They ran at Nyx and piled on top of her, thousands of hounds hopefully suffocating that goddess for good. I didn't want to see her face ever again.

Though I could still feel her power raging through the underworld. She was still alive.

So, I gathered up the tiny bit of strength that I had left. "KILL HER!" I screamed, the words echoing through the forest and vibrating the trees, as my hands collided with the ground to send another wave of energy to the hounds surrounding her.

And then everything went silent. Everything turned dark.

I couldn't feel her power drifting through the air anymore. Now, I could feel it in me.

CHAPTER 42

ARES

"We must kill her now," I said to Marcel, pacing around the prison.

Less than five minutes ago, the hounds had stopped howling and growling. Up above, everything was eerily quiet. Too quiet. The kind of quiet that struck fear right into *my* bones—and I feared close to nothing.

Marcel stood across from Hella with his arms crossed and his jaw clenched. Since he had been down here, Marcel had changed in many ways. His spirit had been broken, and he had become the silent type too. He used to be so outgoing and arrogant.

Hella had silenced him.

"Only Nyx has the power to kill a god," Marcel said, shaking his head. "We can't."

But that wasn't true. Nyx couldn't be the only one who was strong enough to kill a god or goddess. *How did she get that power in the first place? How was she able to kill Aurora the first time around?*

"Let me out," Hella growled.

I glanced over at her small frame, bound in chains that were powerful enough to suppress even a god's power. While she had her shoulders pushed back and her back straight—as if the chains weren't affecting her—her eyes were just a bit dimmer than they had been only moments ago, and there were *darkening* circles under them.

She could pretend all she wanted, but these chains were hurting her.

"The chains," I whispered, matching the pieces together and finally realizing that it wasn't just Nyx who could weaken and kill a divine being. I stepped closer to Hella and crouched to her level. "These were the chains you had Aurora locked inside of as you killed her."

Like a madwoman who had a death wish, Hella grinned wickedly. "Yes."

"Did you make them with your own power?" I asked, though I already knew the answer.

If she had made them with her own power, then she would've escaped them already. I wanted her to start talking, to start rambling. I needed information on how they'd killed Aurora the first time around, so I knew how to make sure something like that could *never* happen again. I refused to feel any more pain.

Fuck saving the world. I'd choose my mate over anyone.

If that made me a villain, then I'd be the greatest fucking villain to ever live.

"I took part in creating them," she boasted, showing me her pearly-white teeth. "They were created in the deepest and lowest pits of the underworld, where only gods can survive."

"Where only gods can survive, huh?" I asked, grabbing one and tugging on it.

Hella moved toward me to ease the pain of the chain on her skin. Around the chains, her skin was turning black, her flesh rotting away. We needed to kill her now, so I could make it back to Aurora in the forest. I needed to find her again.

"What are you getting at?" Marcel asked, running a hand through his long white-silver hair.

"Find me more chains," I said through the mind link, hoping he'd hear me.

Marcel stayed completely still and quiet, as if he hadn't heard what I said through our mind link. Then, he glanced up at the door to the prison, where someone banged harshly. The door rattled uncontrollably, and I knew we couldn't wait any longer.

"Find me more chains now, Marcel!" I growled. "Forget whoever is at the door. I'll handle them if they come in. Grab me as many of these chains as possible. We're going to kill a goddess tonight."

Hella suddenly scurried away from me, the chain searing her skin. "You can't! It's impossible!"

"It's impossible for you," I growled, watching Marcel nod and scurry into another room. "It's impossible for a weak, pathetic woman like *you*. But we're going to kill you tonight. We're going to end your life and your reign for good. I don't care what it takes."

Hella stared at the door, cheeks red. "My hounds will come in and eat you alive."

"Let them try," I growled. "They're not your hounds anymore. You don't control them."

"I do!" Hella shouted, but she sounded too desperate for me to believe her. "I do!"

"Marcel! The chains. Now."

A couple moments later, Marcel hurried into the room and dragged four more chains that radiated power that even burned my skin—and I wasn't even touching them. He dropped them at my feet and swallowed. "You think this will kill her?"

"It has to."

Though I wasn't sure. But if what I thought was correct—that she'd used the chains to weaken Aurora and then let Nyx kill her with her power—then I would weaken Hella enough so that *I* could kill her with my anger.

I took the first chain and wrapped it around Hella's body tightly. Then, I did the same with the second. Then, the third. When I picked up the fourth chain, Hella's body was burning quickly from the intense pain. Her cheeks had sunken in, her eyes not as bright anymore.

"Stop it!" she shouted, voice hoarse. "Stop it now, or you'll be cursed to live in the underworld forever!"

Clenching my jaw, I stepped closer to her and wrapped the fourth chain around her body. She seized in the middle of the chains, shaking her head back and forth and crying out loud like the motherfucking baby that she was.

"Shut your fucking mouth," I gritted out.

Marcel stepped forward, brows furrowed. "What are you talking about?"

"You'll die here!" she screamed. "Whoever kills me will take on my power and be cursed to the underworld forever! Do you want that?! Do you want to never see that bitch you call a mate again?! Never want to see your family back home again?! You'll have to kill innocent people to survive down here. Do you want that?!"

CHAPTER 43

ARES

"What the fuck is she saying?" I asked Marcel, crossing my arms over my chest and watching her burn in fucking hell. I hated this bitch so much that I couldn't think of anything other than her dying pathetically.

Marcel opened and shut his mouth four times. Four fucking times. Then, he finally swallowed and looked at me. "It might be true." He paced around the room and shook his head. "I've read about something like it in her library. When a god dies, whoever kills them will gain their power and their curses. I thought it was nothing more than a fable."

"It's true," Hella gritted out between whimpers. "How do you think Nyx was able to control the hellhounds and the hounds from the Sanguine Wilds? Aurora ... that bitch had complete control of all beings that were active during the dawn and dusk during her first life. When Nyx killed her, they followed Nyx instead."

"But you have control of the hounds too," I said. "Don't fuck with us!"

"I can only raise them from the dead. I don't control them!"

I glanced over at Marcel, unsure if we should believe her. I didn't want to believe a fucking thing that she said, but I didn't know the extent of her power. It would've been nice to be able to raise animals and friends from the dead, to give them a second life. But what if we really couldn't leave the underworld?

"What are your curses?" I asked.

"My curses?" She gave a wicked laugh and shook her head. "My curse is that I can never leave the underworld for more than a few hours a year. I am bound to the underworld for eternity. And if you kill me, you will be too."

Everything seemed to slow down. My stomach tightened and dropped. I clenched my jaw, memories and thoughts racing through my mind. If I couldn't leave the underworld, then I would never be able to see my daughter grow up. I wouldn't get to spend time with Aurora. My life as I knew it would be over.

"If that's what you want, then do it," she said. "Land a final attack on me and kill me."

Jaw twitching, I clenched my fists. All I wanted to do was end her life right here and right now. But I ... I couldn't do that to Aurora and our daughter. They had both been through so much, and we were so close—so fucking close—to defeating Hella for good and getting back home.

"Do it!" she screamed. "Do it or let me go!"

I glanced over at Marcel, who didn't look up from Hella's pathetic figure once. His silver hair was in his face, so I couldn't read his expression.

He shook his head, hands balled into fists by his sides. "You took so much from me," he ground out to her. "Made me feel like nothing. Nothing!"

Marcel stepped forward, and I knew he'd kill her. I knew he'd end her life and be bound here forever, but he needed to think about Charolette. If I didn't come back with him when we got home, she wouldn't only hate me, but she'd also hate him for eternity.

So, I stepped behind him and wrapped my arms around his waist to hold his struggling figure back. "Think about Charolette! Marcel, don't be stupid!"

But instead of listening to me, Marcel ripped himself out of my hold and sprinted toward Hella. "Everything I do is for Charolette. *This*"—he landed a blow directly on Hella's face—"*is to protect her from Hella's wrath.*"

And as his fist collided with her face, Hella's body turned into small particles of dust. Her chains clattered against the stone ground as the dust drifted through the air and created a dark mist. It swayed back and forth like a spirit or a being for a moment and then rushed into Marcel's raging body.

He inhaled the spirit, his blue eyes turning dark, black streaks appearing in his hair, and his lips turning a shade of gray. Marcel's misty body became solid again, hardening and becoming stronger like it'd once been.

"Marcel," I whispered, completely in shock, "what did you do?"

He clenched his jaw. "My mate isn't as strong as Aurora. She can't protect herself, so I did what I could to ensure that nobody will ever hurt her again. And if they do, then I will give them a death that everyone will remember."

"But—"

"Now, leave," Marcel growled, his hard eyes glaring right through me. "Go home with Aurora. Live your life in the Sanguine Wilds. See your daughter. And tell Charolette that I sacrificed myself for the greater good. Tell her that you couldn't stop me. Tell her that I love her."

And while I wanted Marcel to come up to the Sanguine Wilds to see Charolette with me, I knew that would never be possible again. Marcel was bound to the underworld forever. He would live like this forever.

"I'll tell her that you're the greatest hero I know," I said, pulling him into a hug and trying hard not to shed a tear. Marcel had been with me since we were kids, and now, I'd have to live without him. "The greatest hero that I've ever fucking known."

CHAPTER 44

AURORA

Strong, warm arms wrapped around my torso. I lay on the cold forest floor, my body feeling so heavy and my mind reeling with thoughts and dreams and images that were not my own. They looked almost like the future, almost like a piece of everyone's future.

"Kitten," Mars whispered into my ear, lifting me into the air. "Kitten, tell me you're okay."

I squeezed my eyes closed and pressed a hand to my forehead, whimpering softly. "My head hurts," I started, a sharp pain shooting through my temple. When I reopened my eyes, everything looked fuzzy and distant. "I-I can't see."

While my vision became even more far off and blurry, I could feel the wind whipping around my body, as if Mars was rushing through the forest.

"Stay with me, Kitten," he said, his words more and more distant. "I'm going to find Acesca for you."

When my vision became completely black, a bright figure

appeared in the distance. I focused on her, wanting—no, needing —to see, desperate for something that'd help calm my racing heart. All I could think about was that killing Nyx had been a mistake because now, I had lost my sight.

THE FIGURE STARED *at a bonfire burning in the distance with a bunch of wolves around it. Elder wolves—including who looked to be Alpha Vulcan and his warriors—were gathered around it, drinking beer and talking to a muscular, younger alpha wolf about how he should've been mated already, about how he needed a strong luna to lead this pack with him, about how only a she-wolf with beta or alpha blood would do.*

The younger wolf sighed deeply through his nose, staying quiet. A woman—who looked like a spitting fucking image of Mars, Ares, and me—peeked her head around the tree to watch the young wolf nod toward the elders, silently agreeing.

The girl, who must've been our daughter, clutched the tree hard, her claws digging into the bark and her canines lengthening. She gritted her teeth. "Why is he such an asshole? I hate him so much. How could he just agree with them like that?!"

Just from the mere look on her face, I could tell that she was hurting as much as I had that one night that Ares almost ripped my best friend to shreds and hunted me down after I ran away from him. She walked out from behind the trees and looked at the alpha wolf for the briefest moment. A pained expression crossed his face before it was replaced with a devious expression that only Ares had given me before.

They were mates. They had to be.

But instead of our daughter walking over to him, she pulled her gaze away from him and walked to the guy who sat to his right. "Meet me south of the lake, Axel. Five minutes," she whispered.

Axel glanced up at her, his eyes dancing with excitement. He ran his fingers over hers.

The alpha's gaze hardened, watching her fingertips run up Axel's chest. She smiled at him, and for good measure, she pressed a kiss on

Axel's neck. She glanced back up at the alpha to see him clenching his jaw, eyes flashing gold. Then, she balled her hands into tight fists, as if she was simmering with anger, and walked into the forest.

"Aurora!" someone shouted to my left.

I snapped out of the daydream that had been drifting through my mind. I couldn't tell if it was the future or if that had been in real time, but I … I couldn't help but cry out. Whatever it was, all I wanted was to get home soon to see my daughter. This wasn't fair. None of this was fair.

"Aurora," Mars said again, hovering over me now.

With my back against the stone ground, I stared up at the sky and my warriors, who stood around me. I closed my eyes for another brief moment, letting out a long sigh after not seeing another dream, and sat up. I didn't know what was happening to me.

Nyx was gone, dead.

How can I still see them?

"Sit back," Acesca said, gently pushing me back down. "Tell me what happened. You were out for a good five minutes."

"I …" I lay back down against Mars and took another deep breath. "I think I saw the future or the present. I had another one of those dreams about our daughter."

"But we killed Nyx," Mars said in a whisper.

I glanced around the group, hearing whispers and seeing figures that weren't there, but that seemed to be partners or children of these wolves and hounds.

I clutched my head again. "I don't know. I just … I want to go home. We need to find Ares."

CHAPTER 45

MARS

"*P*lease, just take me to see Ares," Aurora said, staring up at me with less haze in her eyes.

My heart hurt as I stared down at the want and desperate need on her face. It felt like an eternity since I had last seen Ares, and I had been wanting to find him too.

We might've been two different people, but we belonged together. We inhabited one body and shared one mate, who loved both of us for who we were. I just didn't know if we would be able to … join up again.

Much time had passed since our personalities had physically split. And personalities *never* split like *this* with humans. No research had been done about us, and none had been done about us merging back together. Is it even possible?

"I want us to be a family again," she whispered. "Please."

After tucking some hair behind her ear, I smiled gently at my mate and helped her to her feet. "Let's go find Ares and get back home to our daughter." I glanced around at all the people who had come down to the underworld with us. "And get you all back to your families as well."

"But, Aurora—" Acesca started.

"It's fine," I said to her. "She just needs her mates again. She'll be fine."

But I wasn't sure if what I had said was the truth or not. I didn't know the first thing about what Aurora had experienced and didn't understand how she could still see those dreams and thoughts after she'd killed Nyx.

Once I took Aurora's hand, I headed toward Hella's castle. Unlike when we'd arrived, this place looked eerily desolate, which hopefully meant that Ares had defeated Hella without much of a problem. At least, I hoped because Aurora didn't have any energy left inside her to fight.

And we were so close to heading back home.

As we made it to the edge of the castle, someone opened a side door. *"Kitten."*

Aurora snapped her head toward our right and stared at Ares, who looked exactly like me, except his body wasn't ghostlike, like mine, but solid. Aurora let go of my hand and ran over to Ares, letting him pick her up into his arms and be spun around in circles.

When he placed her down onto her feet, he looked over her shoulder at me. I stood there for a good long while, just fucking grinning like a dumbass because for the first time in what seemed like forever, he was back.

"It's been a long fucking time," Ares said to me.

I smiled, my heart finally feeling at rest. "A long time."

Aurora pulled away from him and tugged him over to me, glancing between us and smiling. Unable to stop myself, I wrapped my arms around his shoulders and hugged that man tight. He had been with me for so long that when I'd died, I'd lost a part of myself.

We both had.

As we touched, I slowly felt my ghostlike body dipping into his, almost becoming one again, but not fully compatible at the moment.

"Do you think you'll ever be one again?" Aurora whispered, staring between us.

We looked at each other for another moment until I said, "Maybe one day."

After Aurora grinned, Ares pulled her into another long hug, his arms wrapping around her shoulders, and his body finally relaxed for once. He had always been tense and pent up with anger, but tonight … he looked like he was at peace with everything.

"It's time to go home," I said to Aurora, grabbing her hand and guiding her to the others. "To find our daughter."

CHAPTER 46

ARES

$\mathcal{A}$ day later, we stood at the river's base, where we had entered the underworld. Today, we were going home. Home—where I had been born into Mars's body, where I had met Aurora, where this had all started.

"I don't know if I'll be able to leave," Mars said to Aurora, stopping just short of Charon's ferry that led back to the area where Medusa had spawned us in so long ago.

Hades had advised us to head over the river and that Medusa would be waiting for us to get back home.

"What do you mean?" Aurora whispered, curling her fingers against Mars's chest, her eyes watering. "You have to be able to come home. I'm not going anywhere without you. You-you have to come with us."

"I'm nothing but a spirit," Mars said, glancing down at his misty body.

Someone cleared her throat behind us. "You'll be able to make it back home."

I glanced over my shoulder to see Medusa. The snake-like wolves slithered around her head like hair, her eyes were a piercing green, and her skin was aging slowly. I gritted my teeth and grabbed Aurora's other hand, knowing that she would kill Medusa right here and now if I didn't control her.

Aurora growled, canines lengthening. "If you weren't our ticket home, I would kill you."

Medusa gave Aurora, her daughter, a smile. "I know."

Deep down, I thought that Aurora might actually kill her once we got home. We had lost so many years of our daughter's life, being down in the underworld, and Aurora hadn't even gotten to see our daughter's face once.

"Will I be able to survive in the Sanguine Wilds?" Mars asked her.

He didn't know what Medusa had done to Aurora.

"Yes," Medusa said, addressing him directly and ignoring Aurora seething beside him. Medusa turned toward the group of wolves who would be entering back into the real world with her help. "Now, is this everyone that will be traveling with us?"

Mars grabbed Aurora's hand from off his chest, squeezed it, and grinned at us. I gave him a small smile and nodded. We might've been the same yet different people in the past, but ... man, I loved that kid.

I had done everything in my power to protect him for as long as I could, and he had become a man, so much stronger and smarter than me. He had matured from that little boy who needed protection from the monster we called Fenris.

"We have a prisoner too," Mars said, glancing over his shoulder at the group of warriors guarding Fenris. He looked over at me and nodded back, as if to say that he wanted to be the one who tortured Fenris until he died. "We're bringing him to our home, and we're going to give him everything he deserves."

Once Aurora said her goodbye to the gods of the underworld, all the hellhounds, and the hounds who'd stay here once we left, she stepped forward and crossed her arms. "I'll consider not killing you once we make it to the Sanguine Wilds if you keep a portal open from the underworld to the Sanguine Wilds, so the hounds can come visit me anytime they'd like."

After Medusa scanned the group, she nodded. "Fair."

Aurora gritted her teeth, jaw twitching. "Fine."

Medusa called the others to come closer and then mumbled something in a lost, ancient language. My body began hardening, my skin and bones and muscles stiffening like they had the first time she brought us back down here.

One moment passed, then another, and then I couldn't move.

Everything turned dark, black even, like we were in the middle of a black hole. Then, suddenly, the world lit up, and the scent of pine drifted through my nose.

We stood in the middle of the Sanguine Wilds, back home.

As people dispersed around us, Aurora, Ruffles, and Mars stayed behind with me. Aurora smiled at me, her mind racing with thoughts that she couldn't seem to control.

"Our daughter," she whispered to us. "We have to go find her."

"Too late," someone said to our left. "We've already found you."

We all glanced over at Alpha Vulcan and a young man, who was a spitting image of him, which must've been his son. But … Vulcan and his mate couldn't have kids—at least, that was as far as I knew. If it was his son, he had to be at least eighteen years old, which meant that …

A young woman pushed her way through the warriors and finally emerged next to Vulcan and his son, her brown hair flowing in the breeze. Aurora stared at her, one hand over her mouth to hold back a sob as she grabbed on to me tightly.

"My baby," she cried, suddenly throwing her arms around our daughter and pulling her into a tight hug. "I'm sorry. I'm so sorry for not being there for you. I love you so much. So fucking much, sweetheart."

While my mate embraced our daughter, I could do nothing but stare in awe.

Never in my life had I thought I would find someone who would ever love me enough to have my child, and never in my life had I thought I would ever love anyone more than Aurora.

But we had done everything for our daughter. Everything.

And now, we could finally meet her.

Our daughter awkwardly patted Aurora's back, and then she pulled away and glanced up at me. "I … I don't know what to say," she whispered, nervously playing with her fingers. She finally held out her hand. "Ruffles told me everything about what you've done for me."

"Ruffles?" Aurora said, glancing down at our cat. "What do you mean? She came down to the underworld with us."

"She was up here for me," our daughter said. "At least, some days."

Ruffles rubbed her furry body against me and glanced up at us with a mischievous look in her eyes. That cat had secrets that even Aurora didn't know about, secrets that we would never even figure out.

"What's your name?" Mars asked our daughter, directing the attention away from our mischievous cat.

She smiled. "Harper."

"Harper," I whispered, grinning to myself and finally feeling complete for once.

Our daughter's name was Harper.

EPILOGUE

AURORA

"*D*o you think Harper's ever going to come around?" I whispered, curling my arm around Mars's bicep and following my mates down the long hallway of my old pack house.

My brother's, Jeremy, pictures still hung on the walls from when *Mother* lived here.

Every time I passed one, I admired the warrior who had sacrificed so much for me and for the werewolf species. Though he would never live another day in this world, nor the underworld, he deserved to be here and to be remembered.

"Harper spent eighteen years of her life without us," Ares started from my left. "It's going to take her some time to get used to having us around. She's her own woman with her own mate now."

It had been a month since we'd returned from the underworld, and we were slowly settling into the pack house again. So much time had seemed to pass since we had left the Sanguine

Wilds, but things were actually starting to get back to normal—whatever that meant. Our lives were never *really* normal with the hounds constantly hunting us.

"It isn't our fault that we couldn't be here for her," I whispered, chest tightening. "It's Medusa's. I'm glad that she hasn't shown her face around here since she brought us back from the underworld because I wouldn't freaking—"

Mars squeezed my hand with his larger, more solid one. "Calm down, Kitten."

As soon as we had come back to the Sanguine Wilds, his ghostlike body wasn't as transparent anymore. He couldn't walk through walls and float through the air, and his body was becoming his own again.

But Ares …

I glanced over at Ares's fading body and smiled small when he smirked at me with those lustful eyes. Ares was a different story, and I didn't know what was happening to him. To me, it didn't make any sense why their bodies were transforming the way they were. But to them, everything seemed normal.

Or at least, that was the way that Ares had put it last night to me when I asked him about it.

"You know what you do to us when you get all riled up like that, Kitten," Ares growled.

My lips curled into a deeper smile, and my cheeks flushed. "Fine. Fine."

It wasn't fine because Medusa had taken eighteen years of my daughter's life away from me, but I couldn't be salty about it in front of Harper. I just wanted to appreciate the time I had with her now and learn how to be a mother to her.

When we reached the dining hall doors, I stopped in front of them and took a deep breath. Our lives might've been changed forever when we had met, but I wouldn't want it any other way.

Suddenly, the doors flung open.

"What are you guys waiting for?!" Charolette said, eyes gleaming brightly.

She grabbed my wrist and yanked me into the room, where Harper, her mate, and Vulcan sat, ready to feast. Charolette's natural brown hair shimmered under the bright lights. It seemed like she didn't need to wear a wig anymore. Her real hair was silky smooth and thicker than ever.

Small wrinkles fluttered out from the corners of her eyes, and I didn't know if she had gotten them these past eighteen years from smiling and laughing and enjoying life or for crying her eyes out over the disappearance of her mate.

Nevertheless, I pulled her into a hug, like it was the last one that I'd ever give her, and sat down across from my daughter at the dining table. Mars and Ares both sat on either side of me, placing their hands on my thighs and squeezing as if they were still the same person with the same thoughts.

"So," Charolette said, staring between us three, "have you heard anything from the underworld?"

I glanced over at Mars and chewed on my inner lip. "No."

Her eyes glazed over. "Not even from Marcel?" she whispered.

"I told you before, Charolette," Ares said, voice hardening. "Marcel is dead. He's not coming home."

While the tears piled in Charolette's eyes, she shook her head and looked down at her empty plate. "No," she said. "I don't believe you. He's still alive out there somewhere, and one day … one day, I'll find him."

Ares clenched his sharp jaw and stayed surprisingly quiet. "He died a hero."

"He's still alive," Charolette snapped. "I know he is."

"Okay, okay," I interjected, not wanting this to ruin our dinner.

After a few moments of silence, Harper cleared her throat. "So, uh …" She glanced between Ares and Mars. "Are you guys both, like … my dad? How does that even work? Are you guys different people? Brothers?"

"Different personalities in the same body," Mars said, looking over at Ares. "But now, we're, uh"—he chuckled—"kinda different personalities in different bodies."

"We won't be like this forever," Ares said, leaning forward. "One day, we'll return to the same body, but we didn't start like this. Mars had … Mars had been through a rough time when he was a kid—an extremely rough time."

"A lot of trauma," Mars whispered, glancing down at the table and clenching his jaw. "So much that I couldn't handle it alone, and my brain sorta, kinda birthed Ares to protect me from it. He's been here ever since, through everything with me."

"But you've grown into your own," Ares said to Mars. "You don't need me to protect you anymore. You don't need me to fight for you anymore. You've sacrificed more than I ever could to protect our pack."

As Ares continued, his body slowly faded more and more from reality. It was as if he was saying that Mars really didn't need him anymore and that what he had come into this world to do was finally complete. He had fulfilled his destiny.

"You're fading away," I whispered, clutching on to any piece of him that I could touch. "What's happening to you? Don't leave me again. I won't be able to … I can't … I can't do this without you."

Ares brushed his fingers against my cheek. "I'm never leaving you again, Kitten. Don't worry about that. Mars and I are one. We'll always be together, and he'll always give me time with you. Won't you, Mars?"

Mars squeezed my thigh, making me look over at him. His eyes were glimmering gold, like his wolf, yet I could see Ares inside of them too. They were merging back together, someway, somehow.

"I feel stronger than ever, Kitten," Mars said, but it was Ares's voice coming from somewhere deep in Mars's soul.

When I looked over my shoulder to look at Ares, he was gone. And while I should've felt so helpless, I didn't because my mate was back to looking and feeling like himself again.

Mars cleared his throat. "He'll be back out, Kitten." He glanced over at Harper, who stared at us in amazement. "And he'll be back to see you too, Harp. Ares isn't gone for good. Ares just needs time to rest. But, fuck, he loves you both."

The dining hall door opened once more, and Ruffles strutted into the room more dramatically than I had ever seen her. "*Meow!*"

Mars chuckled. "He loves you too, Ruffles. He loves you too."

THE END.

AUTHOR'S NOTE

While this is the end of Ares and Aurora's story, I'm hoping to write a short story about Charolette and Marcel as well as Harper and Kairo! I'm not sure when I'll be writing it, but make sure to follow me for more updates on when to expect it :)

ABOUT THE AUTHOR

Emilia Rose is an international best-selling author of steamy paranormal romance. Highly inspired by her study abroad trip to Greece in 2019, Emilia loves to include Greek and Roman mythology in her writing.

She graduated from the University of Pittsburgh with a degree in psychology and a minor in creative writing in 2020 and now writes novels as her day job.

With over eighteen million combined story views online and a growing presence on reading apps, she hopes to inspire other young novelists with her story of growth and imagination, so they go on to write the stories that need to be told.

STAY CONNECTED

Join Emilia's newsletter for exclusive news > https://www. emiliarosewriting.com/